ONE NIGHT, TWO HOLIDAYS

A CHRISTMAS AND HANUKKAH NOVELLA

ALI BRADY

For anyone who needs a little holiday miracle.

And for Adam Brody. Because, why not?

ALSO BY ALI BRADY

The Beach Trap

The Comeback Summer

Until Next Summer

Battle of the Bookstores

CHAPTER 1

December 24, 2024, 6:23 pm
JACK

*W*hen I booked the last flight on Christmas Eve out of Chicago to Denver, I knew what I was signing up for. I knew I'd be battling traffic and holiday crowds, navigating chaos at O'Hare, making it home just in time for my dad's annual reading of *The Night Before Christmas* while wearing the matching PJ's Mom always buys.

What I didn't plan for was the weather. A record-breaking snowstorm, swirling into the forecast, wreaking havoc on my plans.

I'm standing on the curb in front of my apartment building, swiping furiously at the Uber app on my phone—no one's out driving right now, and I can't blame them. The snow is coming down practically sideways, the wind cutting through my coat and turning my bones to ice.

Shivering, I trudge through the foot of snow on the sidewalk toward the nearest El stop, dragging my carry-on behind me. I force myself to focus on what lies ahead: four precious days of laughter, family, and warmth—an escape from the grind of medical residency. Four days to think about something other than my overwhelming exhaustion, the constant pressure to get everything right, or the crushing sadness of watching patients slip away despite everything we do.

Four days to feel like myself again.

I can almost hear the Christmas music drifting through the house, smell Mom's cookies fresh out of the oven. The thought pulls me forward. I just need to get there. I just need to get *home.*

My phone chimes with a text, and I pull it out of my pocket, swiping away the snowflakes collecting on the screen:

FLIGHT 227 from ORD to DEN has been canceled. Check your email for rebooking options. We apologize for the inconvenience.

Groaning, I flip over to my email inbox, scanning the message that just arrived from the airline, searching for some glimmer of good news: a flight later tonight? Or early in the morning?

But then I read the final line, and it's like an icicle piercing my heart:

Due to severe weather conditions, the Federal Aviation Administration has issued a full ground stop at O'Hare International Airport until further notice.

My chest constricts, and I feel the sting of tears threatening—whether from the wind or sheer frustration, I don't know—and I lean my head back and release a string of profanities toward the snow-streaked sky.

A couple passing with their two kids—both bundled up like marshmallows, an older child holding the mom's hand and a toddler in the dad's arms—glance at me disapprovingly.

"Sorry," I mutter, heat rushing to my face despite the cold.

"Merry Christmas," the woman says, but the way she says it might as well mean *go to hell.*

Pretty sure I'm already there.

Gritting my teeth, I stomp back toward my apartment. The wind howls around me, matching the storm brewing in my chest.

These past six months have been the toughest stretch of my life: moving to a new city where I don't know a soul, working endless hours at the hospital, trying to study whenever I can scrape together a few minutes, all while battling the constant, gnawing worry that I shouldn't even be here. That I, who once thought nothing could rattle me—not facing an icy double black diamond or throwing the last pitch in a championship game—have no business making life-or-death decisions. That I was fooling myself to think I could ever be someone's doctor.

The one thing that's kept me going is the promise of Christmas at home. Instead, I'm marooned in a winter wasteland, freezing and alone.

By the time I reach my building, I'm seething with pent-up agitation, every snow-covered step only adding fuel to the fire. The apartment building looms ahead like a scene from a frozen apocalypse—a snow-choked courtyard surrounded by hulking buildings, their darkened windows staring at me like empty eyes. Not a single light shines from any unit.

I barely know my neighbors—no time for small talk and socializing between shifts—but I assume they're all celebrating elsewhere tonight. Or they were smart enough to get out of Chicago before it turned into a giant snow globe of misery. It's the most desolate, cold, and achingly lonely scene I've ever encountered.

That's when I spot them. The snowmen.

Someone must have built them earlier today, probably when this courtyard was still a winter wonderland. Now they stand there like deformed soldiers, their twig arms and lopsided faces mocking me.

With a burst of frustration, I kick the nearest one with my boot, watching it crumble into a pile of sad, icy chunks. A surge of grim satisfaction hits me. With a grunt, I target the next one with a bigger kick, sending its basketball-sized head flying in a flurry of white.

By the time I reach the third snowman, I'm practically vibrating with pure spite. I ball my gloved hand into a fist and smash it right through its smug, lumpy face. Snow explodes around me, and for a brief, ridiculous moment, I feel triumphant.

"Hey!"

A voice echoes from behind me.

I turn to see a light flicker on in one of the windows, illuminating a woman's face, framed by dark hair.

"Should I be worried?" she calls.

Something about her is familiar. I stare up at her, confused, until it hits me: she's the woman I keep seeing around the building. She's hard to miss, with that wild, curly dark hair and big, bright eyes. Just last week, I saw her helping an older couple in our building carry their groceries in, her laughter floating down the hall and bringing a genuine smile to my face for the first time that day.

I've thought about saying something to her more times than I can count. But with my long hours, late nights, and barely any sleep, I haven't had the energy—or the guts—to even try.

"Huh?" I manage, still dazed.

She gestures at the toppled snowmen behind me. "Am I next on your hit list?"

A surprised laugh bursts out of me. "Nah, you're safe—unless you're made of the same stuff ruining my holiday plans."

She laughs, and a flicker of warmth spreads through me, like a candle igniting in the dark.

CHAPTER 2

December 24, 6:47 pm
NESSA

One person's day ruined, another's night made.

I lean further out the window into the bitter cold, wishing I'd tamed my hair, or at least put on lipstick before investigating who or what was making the ruckus in the courtyard. If I'd known it was the man we've been calling Hot New Guy since he moved in last summer, I would have made more of an effort.

Situations like this are exactly why my grandmother always told me not to leave the house without clean underwear. You never know when you're going to get in an accident or have a chance encounter with the man you and your roommates have been low-key stalking for months.

We've barely gathered any intel, but not for lack of trying. Maybe this is the universe's way of throwing me a bone since I didn't have enough money or enough time off to have an actual vacation like my roommates, and my parents are going on an anniversary trip to Cancun rather than visit their only child.

Now, at least I'll have something to contribute to the post-holiday debrief.

"You can't blame the snow for your bad decision," I say, wrapping my sweater tighter around myself. "You should have left town early like everyone else."

"You sound like my mother," Hot New Guy says.

"And every news anchor and meteorologist on TV."

Hot New Guy glares up at me, and even from the courtyard below, his icy blue eyes send a chill down my spine. For a second, I worry I've crossed the line—the guy's clearly having a shitty day—but then the corner of his mouth quirks up, and I can tell he's fighting back a smile.

"Did the snowpocalypse ruin your Christmas plans, too?" he asks.

"I didn't have any Christmas plans to ruin."

Something pity-adjacent flashes across his face—which I want to put the kibosh on immediately. I got enough of that from my roommates before they left, breaking our annual tradition of making latkes, drinking wine, and watching whatever cheesy Hanukkah movie we can find (there's usually at least one for every two hundred Christmas movies).

I'm not upset at them for leaving—hanging out at home with me wouldn't be my first choice for the holidays, either. And I don't blame my parents for choosing Mexico over me—they deserve to celebrate thirty years of marriage. But I can't help but feel the sting of being left behind. By everyone.

"Don't feel bad for me," I tell him, and myself. "It's just not my holiday." I lift my Star of David necklace even though it's too small for him to see from a distance. "I'm Jewish."

"Ah, then happy almost Hanukkah. First time in almost twenty years that the first night is on Christmas."

"You aren't Jewish, are you?" If I had to guess, he looks Irish with his fair complexion and dark hair. But maybe he's dating a Member of the Tribe. "Or you have a Jewish girlfriend. Or boyfriend?" I add, hoping the question in my voice isn't too obvious.

"No girlfriend or boyfriend. Jewish or otherwise."

My fingers twitch, torn between grabbing my phone to text our *Apt 2B (Or Not 2B)* group chat with this hot intel, or risking hypothermia to keep hanging half out the window to get more of it. Of course, I have no choice but to take one for the team. I'll text them all the details later, provided my fingers haven't frozen off.

"I heard someone talking about it at the hospital," Hot New Guy says, "And my brain holds on to random facts—I swear, it's the only reason I passed my boards."

"You're a doctor?" I ask, pretending this is news to me and we haven't clocked him coming in and out of the building wearing scrubs.

"First-year resident in pediatrics," he says. "So, you don't have any plans tonight?"

"I didn't say that—I've got a traditional Jewish Christmas Eve dinner getting cold inside."

"Well, don't let it get colder on my account." He pauses, and I curse myself, realizing my mistake. Before I can come up with a way to resuscitate this conversation, he says, "Have a good night...you didn't tell me your name."

I smile—no reason to ask my name if he doesn't intend to use it. "It's Nessa."

"Like Elphaba's sister?"

My smile grows. "*Wicked* fan?"

"Haven't seen it," he admits. "But I had a patient last week who's obsessed."

"That's sweet, but no—it means miracle in Hebrew."

"That's really pretty." He nods like he's filing that fact away. "I'm Jack, by the way."

"Well, Merry Christmas Eve, Jack. Tell your mom I said not to be too hard on you."

He lifts his hand in a friendly wave before trudging through the snow, past the two snow people he didn't get a chance to decapitate, and into the front door of our building. I shut the window but keep my nose pressed against it, watching for another light to turn on. A few moments later, it does—a corner unit one floor down.

So, Jack lives on the first floor. I smile, adding this little fact to the others. But the warm glow doesn't last long. Without anyone to share the story with, the night suddenly feels even more lonely than it did an hour ago.

CHAPTER 3

December 24, 7:13 pm
JACK

*M*y studio apartment has never screamed "home sweet home"—and usually, I'm not here enough to care. But tonight? It feels downright bleak. I just got off the phone with my parents, and even though they both tried to sound upbeat, I could hear their disappointment. Not that I blame them. I'm crushed, too.

I promised them I'd keep checking the airport status, and as soon as it opens, I'll book the first flight home. With any luck, I'll get a flight out early tomorrow and arrive before our traditional Christmas morning brunch: quiche, cinnamon rolls, and sausage.

My stomach growls, reminding me of how empty I feel inside. I haven't eaten since the free lunch at noon journal club. I open my fridge, only to see a wilted head of lettuce, a dried-out block of cheddar cheese, and some condiment bottles staring back at me. Luckily, I have a few frozen meals in the freezer, so I grab one, stick it in the microwave, and lean against the counter.

My mind drifts to the cute girl upstairs. Nessa. Cute *and* funny.

She was smart to get her dinner order in early, before the snow started piling up—no one's delivering anymore in this weather, that's for sure. Would it be weird to go up and knock on her door?

Super weird, I tell myself. And intrusive. The last thing a woman wants when she's home alone is some guy she's barely spoken to showing up unannounced. Still, I wish I'd gotten to know her sooner, before my life got so...heavy. Before I got so damn tired. My mind conjures an image of us sitting in her apartment, bantering back and forth like we did a few minutes ago.

Maybe after the holidays, when I'm not feeling so beaten down, I'll find some way to talk to her properly.

I'm reaching for a glass of water when the lights snap off, plunging the place into darkness. I blink, confused. Then I open the fridge—no light. The microwave's dead, too.

"You've got to be kidding me," I mutter to no one.

Alone on Christmas Eve, and the power goes out. Could this night get any worse?

Fifteen minutes later, I'm realizing the answer is yes. Yes, it can get worse.

Not only is the power still off, but the cold is creeping in fast. I'd turned the heat down when I thought I'd be leaving, and now, with the wind howling outside, it's dropped close to freezing already. I put on my coat and hat, then wrap myself in the comforter from my bed—the only blanket I've got. I imagine myself slowly freezing through the night, my fingers and toes turning black with frostbite.

Other problems: I don't have any candles, and my phone

battery is down to 42%. If it dies, I'll lose my only light source, and I'll have no way of tracking the airport updates.

Nessa probably has candles—the nice, scented kind, I bet. Something warm and inviting, like vanilla or cinnamon. I don't know why, she just seems like the type who'd keep her place homey and comfortable. I'm sure she has extra blankets, too. And flashlights.

If I have a *reason* to knock on her door, that makes it less weird, right?

Before I can talk myself out of it, I grab my phone and—still wrapped in my blanket—head out my door and up the stairs, then knock on her door.

I'm shivering, hopping from foot to foot, when I hear a voice, muffled.

"Who is it?"

"It's Jack from downstairs. The snowman destroyer?" I grimace at the lame joke. "Not trying to bother you, just wondering if your power's out, too."

Which, duh, of course it is—the entire building is pitch black.

There's a long pause. Just as I start to think I should leave, the door opens a few inches, and there she is. Dark, wavy hair spills over her shoulders, faintly shining in the candlelight behind her. Her face is in shadow, but I catch the gleam of her eyes, and for a second, I forget why I even came up here.

"Yes, my power's out." She sounds amused—probably because I currently resemble a half-frozen burrito.

Behind her, the room looks impossibly cozy—flickering candles, a couch covered in throw pillows and blankets, takeout containers on the coffee table, a book resting on the sofa arm.

Best of all, a gas fireplace sending a golden glow through the room. It's the most inviting thing I've seen in weeks, and I instinctively lean in, drawn to the warmth. Or maybe to her.

How does one say, *Hey, I know we just met, but can I borrow some candles and blankets and maybe even crash here for a bit because my apartment is a frigid, lonely icebox?*

"Of course, sorry," I say, awkwardly shuffling away. "I'll let you get back to your—"

"Do you want to come in?" she blurts.

I turn. She's staring up at me with wide eyes, like she's surprised herself.

My heart gives an unexpected kick. "I'd love to."

CHAPTER 4

December 24, 7:51 pm
NESSA

"*M*ake yourself at home," I say, opening the door wider. Hot New Guy—Jack—looks freezing. His teeth are literally chattering. "Here, sit by the fire and warm up."

He either nods or shivers aggressively and makes a beeline toward the fireplace—one of the main reasons we keep renewing our lease. That and we all agreed it isn't worth the hassle of moving until we can afford a place with an in-unit washer/dryer and a pool. Or until one of us gets married—which felt a lot further away at twenty-three than it does now at twenty-eight.

Jack drops to his knees and holds his open palms up to the glass. He looks like he's praying, and I wonder if the holiday means more to him than Santa Claus, reindeer, and fruitcake. There's something in his posture that looks more than just cold, though—he looks sad, almost defeated.

"Are you okay?" I ask. His teeth are still chattering, and his lips have a blueish tint in the firelight. The power's only been out for about thirty minutes, but who knows how long he was outside in the blizzard before his assault on the snow people.

Jack lets out a shaky breath that sounds so cold it makes me shiver, and I stuff my hands in the pockets of my fleece-lined sweatpants. They're toasty and warm—or maybe that's my body heat? Isn't that the best way to help someone get their body temperature back to normal? Skin-to-skin contact?

I take in his broad shoulders. The blanket is covering the bulk of him, but the memory of the first time I saw him is vivid enough to fill in the blanks.

It was a week or two after the Fourth of July, and I was heading out to a street festival when Jack—then Hot New Guy—was coming in from a run, shirtless. I remember being impressed by his calves, which is not a part of the male anatomy I've ever been particularly drawn to. The other thing I couldn't help but notice was his height—at least six feet tall—and his barely-there chest hair, unlike the NJBs—Nice Jewish Boys—of my past.

I take a tentative step toward him and lay my hands on his back, rubbing wide circles. Maybe the friction will help? Jack makes another noise, this one more like a moan. The sound does something to me, and I do some quick math. It's been eight and a half months since I've had the pleasure of getting off by something that didn't require batteries.

No wonder I'm like a live wire around this guy. I continue making circles on his back until his breathing slows and his body seems to stabilize. Apparently, I have the opposite effect on him as he has on me. Which is for the best anyway, since Julie called dibs on him.

Plus, banging a neighbor is only convenient until somebody decides he "needs space" because you're getting too clingy even though he's the one who knocked on your window literally every night, and then, you have to see him bringing home a different girl every weekend because his front door was literally three feet from yours.

It's the story of my life: I'm either not enough or too much. One or the other, nothing in between. Never anyone's first choice.

"Thank you," Jack says now, and I hope I didn't make things weird. I take a step back, suddenly not sure what to do with my hands.

I stuff them back in my pockets and say, "It's the least I could do—I'm sorry your holiday keeps getting worse."

Jack turns and smiles, a subtle quirk of his lips that makes my inner thermostat turn up a few degrees. "It's starting to get better."

I can tell the moment he clocks the Joy's Noodles take-out bag on the floor. His eyebrows arch, and I follow his gaze to the coffee table where there are enough take-out containers to feed a family of four.

I'm bracing myself for a comment about the copious amount of food I got to properly eat my feelings when he says, "Thai? I thought Jews ate Chinese food on Christmas?"

"We're not a monolith." I don't mean to sound offended, especially because he's right. "But also, I haven't found decent Chinese that delivers around here."

"But you found good Thai?"

"The best. You hungry?"

His stomach answers for him, letting out a low, rumbling grumble. Almost like a growl. I can't help but smile, even though I wish he were hungry for me and not my Pad See Ew.

CHAPTER 5

December 24, 8:47 pm
JACK

*N*essa has the most expressive eyes I have ever seen.

I wonder if she realizes this; I wonder if she knows that her emotions dance in them like candles flickering in a window, illuminating everything beneath the surface.

Like right now, as we sit side by side on the couch and finish off the Thai food she graciously shared with me, she's telling me how her roommates took off for the holiday week—one on a Caribbean cruise, another to visit her boyfriend's family in Michigan. She's smiling, saying it's fine and she doesn't mind, but there's a glimmer of loneliness in those big brown eyes.

"I had a lot of work to get done anyway," she says. She's a copywriter for an advertising agency, she told me earlier, which I thought was very cool, like a modern-day Peggy on *Mad Men*.

"You didn't want to be with family for the holiday?" I've already told her my sad story—though I tried my best to hide how utterly dejected I feel.

She shrugs. "Eh, my parents are on a trip for their anniversary. Plus, Hanukkah isn't a major holiday—it just got commercialized to keep Jewish kids from feeling left out when Santa's making the rounds and everyone else is drowning in tinsel and gift wrap."

"Fair enough. But you probably still have traditions."

I don't know why I'm asking this, maybe because I'm missing *my* family's traditions. But also because of that *something* about her that makes me want to find out more.

"Sure, when I was a kid. My grandma was really into all the holidays—but once she died, we kind of stopped. The last few years, my roommates and I would have a latke night, and we'd play drinking dreidel and watch cheesy movies." She glances at me, smiling, but her eyes tell a different story: she misses the way her family used to be, and the friends who are like family.

I understand completely.

Then she blinks and looks away. "So, is your family a Christmas Eve family or a Christmas Day family?"

"Both," I say, smiling at the memories despite the hollow feeling in my chest. "Christmas Eve dinner, followed by forced family caroling—picture my mom singing *Jingle Bells* off-key while my dad tries to harmonize. Then, we'd put on matching pajamas and watch *It's a Wonderful Life* while drinking my grandma's famous homemade peppermint hot cocoa."

"Sounds delicious."

"It's the best," I say, sighing. "The next morning, we always open stockings first. Mom fills them with the same things every year: a book, Chapstick, chocolates, and a lottery ticket. Weird, but..."

"It's the tradition of it all," she finishes, nodding.

"Exactly. Did you know that people who have strong family traditions are sixty-three percent more likely to report feelings of happiness and contentment on holidays?"

She laughs, shaking her head, and I realize I'm doing the thing

I do when I'm a little nervous: dropping random trivia I've picked up.

"Sorry." I grimace. "I tend to overdo it with the factoids—kids love them, especially when I bust out details about their favorite YouTubers or cartoon characters. But adults, sometimes not so much."

"No, it makes sense," she says, smiling. "There's something magical about doing the same things year after year. Like a thread that ties us all together, a tapestry of memories woven through time."

Warmth spreads through me, and I glance over at her. "That's...beautiful."

And so are you.

The thought flares in my mind like a shooting star, and I press my lips together to keep from accidentally blurting it out. It's not just her eyes—it's her wavy dark hair, the fullness of her bottom lip, the way her oversized sweatshirt keeps slipping off one shoulder to reveal a pink bra strap against lightly freckled skin.

Knock it off, I order myself. I'm in her space, and I'd never want to make her feel uncomfortable—partly because I might freeze to death if I go back to my apartment before the power comes back on.

But mostly because, for the first time in months, I think I'm having...fun?

"Hopefully, the airport opens tomorrow, and you can get a flight home," Nessa says.

If it doesn't, I'll probably curl into a fetal position and sob until I'm hoarse, I think. But I don't say that, of course. Instead, I tell myself to pull it together, to act like the guy I used to be—pre-residency, pre-burnout, when I still had a personality. When I had at least *some* game with cute girls.

"Can't wait to get rid of me?" I say, summoning up a grin.

Her cheeks turn a slight shade of pink. It's surprisingly

adorable—but I can't help but wonder what else would make her blush, where else that warmth could blossom. "No, that's not—"

"I get it." I chuckle. "I'm sure the last thing you wanted tonight was to become a shelter for freezing refugees from downstairs."

She rolls her eyes playfully. "Actually, my roommates and I have been trying to figure out a way to introduce ourselves. To you."

She's noticed me, too? That's…unexpected. Though I couldn't care less about the roommates; I can't even remember what they look like.

"Well," I say, trying to ignore the way my heart picks up a little, "I've been trying to figure out a way to introduce myself to you, too."

"My roommates will be thrilled to hear that."

Her tone is light, casual. But her eyes say something else, flicking down to my mouth and back to my eyes. The air between us seems to crackle with electricity.

I'm struck by the thought that maybe she's not just being polite. Maybe she's not annoyed that I'm here. Maybe she's even a little bit…glad?

I push past the exhaustion weighing me down, forcing myself to be present. To be fun.

"Not your roommates." I lean in a little. "Just you."

Her lips part, surprise flashing across her face. "Oh."

The word hangs in the air, charged with a feeling I can't quite define. For a second, it's like I'm right back in those moments when I've noticed her. I can't pinpoint exactly why, but there's something about her that captures my attention, makes me want to know more.

Then my phone chimes on the coffee table, shattering the spell. I grab it, hoping for an update on my flight:

O'Hare International Airport will remain with a full ground stop until December 25, 2024, at 3:00 pm. Unfortunately, we expect exten-

sive delays and/or cancellations. Further information to be posted by
12:00 pm tomorrow. We apologize for the inconvenience.

"Shit," I mutter.

"What?"

I show her the message, my chest constricting as it hits me that I might not make it home at all. That my four days of vacation might be spent alone in my apartment, riding out this snowstorm, dreading my inevitable return to the hospital. And then it all crashes over me again: the exhaustion, the burnout, the simmering fear that I'm on the wrong path.

"I'm really sorry," she says softly.

"Me, too."

After a beat, she straightens up, determination flashing in those wide brown eyes. "Well, I don't have homemade peppermint hot cocoa, but I have something that might be even better, given the circumstances."

I raise my eyebrows, intrigued. "What's that?"

"Wine."

CHAPTER 6

December 24, 11:10 pm
NESSA

*T*wo hours and almost two bottles of wine later, the power is still out, and my sides hurt from laughing. The booze—and the company—has left me feeling warm and cozy despite the howling wind outside.

We're curled up on the couch, a pile of blankets around us and candles flickering on the coffee table. It would be romantic if we weren't practically strangers. But we're not strangers. We're neighbors.

And after trading stories from the holidays of our childhood, I know more random facts about eight and ten-year-old Jack than I know about my actual friends when they were that age. And the more I get to know him, the more my attraction grows. Yes, he's hot. But he's also really sweet and smart and funny and—

"Ground control to Major Tom."

I blink, and Jack is inches away from my face. It's crazy, but I can't stop thinking about how easy it would be to lean forward and kiss him. It's probably the wine talking. I didn't even know the man three hours ago, plus I have a firm policy against making the first move. I'm still scarred from eighth grade when I totally misinterpreted the signs I *thought* Jason Blumberg was giving me, when he really wanted to ask out my best friend.

But Jack already said he wasn't interested in Julie or Amanda.

Not your roommates. Just you.

Jack reaches out and tucks a stray hair behind my ear, and somehow, that simple gesture feels more intimate than a kiss. "Where'd you go?" he asks.

"The North Pole," I say, resorting to humor like I always do after I make things awkward.

"Ahh," Jack says. He looks delighted and totally game for playing along the way I imagine he does with his patients. "How was it?"

"Honestly, it wasn't as cold as I expected—a few degrees warmer than here."

He shivers, as if being reminded of the cold. "Did you at least see Santa?"

"No, I think he's delivering presents somewhere over France —BUT I did see Mrs. Claus, and I asked her if you were on the naughty or the nice list."

Jack's eyebrows arch. "And what did she say?"

"Surprisingly, she said you were on the nice list. I was sure she'd say naughty...."

My eyes dip down to his lips again, and my mind wanders to all the places I'd like to feel them, pressed against my own lips, my shoulder, my breast...

What has gotten into me? I set my glass of wine down; I must be tipsier than I thought.

Jack must be tipsy, too. He's giving me what I can only describe as bedroom eyes. "Oh, I'm very nice..."

"Unless you happen to run across a snowman."

Jack laughs. "If you knew me, you'd know how out of character that was."

If I knew him? Point taken. I pull my knees against my chest, a reminder to stay on my side of the couch. I don't know him, and he doesn't know me. We're two strangers marooned on a couch in the middle of the worst snowstorm to hit Chicago in a century.

I clear my throat. "Well, the good news is that Santa seems to agree—so you won't be getting coal this year."

Jack's face falls, and it's like someone popped the balloon on our party.

"I'm sorry, I didn't mean to make you sad."

He sighs. "It's okay—and it's not about the actual presents— but like you said, the tradition of it all."

"The stockings," I say, remembering what he told me earlier. We may not have lottery tickets, but I have an idea.

I throw the blanket off me, startling Jack. The wood floor is cool on my bare feet as I hurry down the hall toward Amanda's room. I find just what I'm looking for in her top dresser drawer and quickly hurry back to the living room, dangling one of her compression socks from each hand.

Jack's expression goes from confused to delighted as I say, "Wanna stuff my stocking?"

CHAPTER 7

December 24, 11:49 pm
JACK

*N*essa's idea to stuff stockings for each other has been the perfect distraction. She suggested that we fill them with random objects that carry some kind of meaning, and we'll open them together in the morning.

The only problem? My apartment is a barren wasteland and I'm struggling to find anything decent to put in hers.

Also, it's pitch dark and freezing in here. Armed with one of Nessa's emergency flashlights, I'm rummaging around my place, searching for anything that might bring a smile to her face. For some reason, it feels important that I get this right. And not just because she's been so generous, letting me hang out with her during the power outage.

But because of this…whatever it is between us. The simmering attraction I can't ignore. I tried to stay on my side of the couch while we were talking, but I kept catching myself shifting toward her, pulled by some magnetic force. And every time, the same thought kept popping in my head:

How would she react if I kissed her?

Do not kiss her, I order myself as I sift through my dresser drawers. What if these sparks I'm feeling are just delusional hopes fueled by the wine and good conversation, plus how kind she's being (and yes, how pretty she is) on a miserable night? I would feel like garbage for overstepping.

But if she kissed me...I'd kiss her back in a heartbeat. No question.

FIFTEEN MINUTES LATER, I've managed to gather a few things for her stocking, though I'm not at all sure they'll be good enough. But the compression sock is bulging and I'm officially frozen, my toes numb, my nose stinging from the cold.

When I open the door to Nessa's apartment, it's like stepping into a hug from the world's coziest sweater. She's by the fireplace, hanging the other sock on the mantle with a removable sticky hook; there's an empty hook next to it.

She turns, smiling, but her expression falters when she sees my face. "What happened?"

"So. Cold." I shiver, hurrying over to the fire for the second time this evening.

She takes the sock from me and hangs it next to the other one. Then she grabs a blanket from the sofa, and for a second, I think she's going to toss it my way.

But then she stops, wraps the blanket around herself, and opens it up like she's inviting me to come inside.

"You need to warm up," she says, almost shyly.

I don't need any more encouragement. I step closer, and she wraps the blanket around us both, sealing us in a cozy cocoon. Her head tucks under my chin, and my arms find their way around her, pulling her closer.

Relaxation rushes through me, like a tightly wound knot slowly loosening in my chest. She feels *so* good. Curvy, soft, and warm, like she was made to fit right here. I press my nose to the top of her head, breathing in the sweet scent of her hair. I haven't been this close to another human in months. The last hug I got was probably from my mom before I left on the plane here.

My eyes sting, and I blink furiously. No way in hell am I letting the prettiest woman I've met in ages see what a fucking mess I am right now.

"Better?" she asks, her voice muffled against my chest.

"Much better. Should've done this hours ago, though."

She laughs, and her breath tickles my neck, sending a pleasant shiver down my spine. "Do you want to go sit on the couch again?"

"Hmmm." I pretend to consider that. "I mean, I would, but I'm worried that if I let go of you to move over there, I might freeze."

She lets out another laugh. "We'll just have to stay wrapped up in the blanket, then."

Together, we shuffle over to the couch, our feet tangling in the blanket as we struggle to make it without tripping. When my legs hit the sofa, I fall backward in an awkward heap, pulling Nessa with me. She squeals, and I laugh, shifting around to lie on my back—and nearly rolling her off the edge.

"Watch out," I say, wrapping an arm around her and pulling her back.

I expect her to sit up, put some space between us, but instead she curls a little closer, resting her cheek carefully on my chest.

"This okay?" she murmurs, tucking the blanket around us.

An unexpected vision slams into me: holding her like this, with nothing between us—no cozy sweaters, no blankets, just skin on skin. I swallow, shaking that thought away, and put an inch of space between our bodies so it's just her head on my chest, my arm around her shoulders. "Yeah. It's great."

We settle into a comfortable silence, listening to the fire crackling in the background and the sound of each other's breathing. The warmth of her body radiating toward mine, the blanket around us—I could stay like this forever, suspended in this quiet, peaceful moment.

"So, I'm thinking," she says after a bit. "You should probably sleep here tonight."

My heart swoops like I've just stepped off a cliff, but I force myself to sound casual. "As long as you're okay with that."

"I mean, what would I tell your mom if you froze to death on Christmas?"

"Guess that would make for a pretty awkward phone call."

My hands ache with the urge to touch her—to trace the curve of her waist, to cup her jaw and pull her lips to mine. But she seems content to stay just like we are, so I force myself to hold still, to ride out the tension that builds and subsides in waves.

All too soon, my eyelids grow heavy. The world beyond the firelight fades away, and with it, all the pressure, the exhaustion, the noise of my regular life.

And without realizing it, I drift off to sleep

CHAPTER 8

December 25, 8:10 am
NESSA

I can feel the sun before I see it. It's so cozy here, cocooned in the warmth of blankets and...my eyes fly open, and I remember where I am. Snuggled up on the couch with Hot New Guy—Jack—spooning me. And that hard object pressed against my back is his—

"Merry Christmas!" I shout, leaping up from the couch.

Jack startles awake, rubbing his eyes. He opens the left one, looking at me like I've lost my mind. His dark hair is a spiky mess, and there's a hint of stubble on his jaw.

"What?" I ask. "Isn't this what you do on Christmas morning? Wake up early to open all your presents?"

"Not this early." He props himself up on his elbow. "And not before coffee."

"Power's still out—so I can't help with the coffee. But we do have presents!" I hold my hand out, presenting the stockings we filled for each other last night.

"Are you always this peppy in the morning?" he asks, sitting straight up.

I swallow down the implication—I'm being extra—and attempt to shrug the thought away. "It's my first Christmas. Of course I'm excited—how does it work with the stockings? Do we pour all the presents out or go one at a time?"

A smile tugs at the corner of Jack's mouth, and if I didn't know better, I'd think he might be charmed by my enthusiasm. "Bring them here, we can take turns. But fair warning—I didn't have much handy. I had to get creative."

"Perfect. Especially because it's the thought that counts—and creativity takes extra thought!" I unhook the stockings and lay them on the coffee table before taking my spot on the couch next to Jack. "We need music—how's your battery?"

Jack grabs his phone and frowns. He holds it up, showing the black screen. "Long gone. Yours?"

I reach for mine. "Twenty percent. Enough for a little holiday cheer." I open Spotify to search for a Christmas morning playlist until Jack stops me, putting his hand on mine.

As his skin touches mine, a jolt of electricity runs through me. I look down at his fingers, splayed across the back of my hand. I can't remember ever feeling anything like this before from such a simple touch. The last time I felt anything close to this...well, it definitely wasn't my hand being touched.

I look up at Jack, who seems just as perplexed by whatever it is that's happening between us. His blue eyes sparkle, full of unspoken questions. I want to tell him yes, but I need him to ask. To initiate.

Keeping my eyes locked on his, I turn my hand over so we're palm-to-palm. Practically holding hands.

"Is it worth the risk?" Jack asks.

My heart hammers in my chest, and I honestly can't think of a single risk I wouldn't take to be with this man. Yes, the whole neighbor thing makes it complicated. And Julie did call dibs on him—but she's on a cruise, and I'm here. With Jack sitting kiss-ably close.

I'm about to tilt my head in invitation when he says, "Your battery."

Confused, I sit back. "My...what?"

"We don't know how long the power will be out," Jack says, looking down at our hands on my phone.

My cheeks warm as I realize what he's talking about. *This* is why I don't trust my judgment with men.

"Is it worth burning what's left of your battery to play some cheesy Christmas music?" he asks.

"First of all, yes." I remove my hand from his. "Second of all, have a little faith. Hanukkah is the Festival of Lights, it's a holiday of miracles. The power will be back on before my phone dies."

"You think?"

I shrug. "I think it's worth the risk." I hit play and Mariah Carey comes blasting out the small speakers, singing words that have never been more true: In this moment, all I want for Christmas is Jack.

Too bad I have absolutely no clue whether or not he wants me, too.

THIRTY MINUTES LATER, we're down to the last gifts at the bottom of our stockings.

Jack understood the assignment; each gift I've opened so far, while nothing extraordinary, has felt special and chosen for me. Like he's actually gotten to know me over these last twelve hours.

He gave me a notebook from one pharmaceutical company and a pen from another to use for my ideas at work (he paid attention when I told him what I did!), a Ventra card for our next adventure (he wants to hang out with me again!), a full punch-card from the coffee shop down the street valid for a free drink (yum!), a lucky penny so I could make a wish, and a mug that says "myocardium belongs to you," which he explained was a more technical way of saying his heart.

In Jack's stocking, I put a scarf that one of Julie's hookups left here a few weeks ago, a fortune cookie from last night, a bookmark, a dollar so he could buy a scratch-off when the stores open back up, some breath mints, a vanilla candle since he said he didn't have any, hand sanitizer and a pair of chopsticks.

"Last gifts," Jack says, rubbing his hands together. "Want to go first?"

"No, you."

Jack's face lights up as he reaches back into his compression sock, and I get a flash of what he must have been like as a little boy on Christmas morning. It makes me wish I had something a little more special to give him.

He pulls out the last item—a bag of Hershey Kisses.

"Almost exactly what I was hoping for." His eyes drift down to my lips, and my stomach does a little flip.

"I mean, they're not as good as the real thing," I say. Which is about as forward as I can bring myself to be.

He gives me a slow nod, one eyebrow quirking. "I'll keep that in mind."

A little flustered, I reach into the compression stocking and grab what feels like a slip of paper, an oversized Post-it. I pull it out, and it takes me a second to recognize it as a prescription pad. There's something scribbled on the front—and true to the stereotype, Jack's handwriting is awful.

I bring the paper closer and try to make out the words—back something?

"It says good for one back rub," Jack says, laughing. "I told you I had to get creative."

"I love it—it's almost exactly what *I* was hoping for," I say, echoing his words. I wonder if this is his "creative" way of saying he wants to touch me. Turning toward him on the couch, I let my knee brush against his. Jack doesn't move, and neither do I. "This has been the best Christmas ever."

"It's your only Christmas," he reminds me.

"My first, but hopefully not my last. So, what's next on our Christmas morning agenda?"

Jack doesn't hesitate: "Breakfast."

CHAPTER 9

December 25, 10:26 am
JACK

*S*ince the power's still out, breakfast options are limited —no fresh cinnamon rolls or quiche happening this morning. But one perk of being snowed in is that the kitchen's the temperature of a refrigerator, so at least everything in there is preserved.

We settle for cold cereal with milk, a smorgasbord of random snacks from Nessa's cupboards, and a puzzle. Apparently, one of Nessa's roommates has a whole stash of them, so when I mention my dad's tradition of tackling a new 1,000-piece jigsaw puzzle every Christmas, she lights up and pulls out one featuring a vintage Chicago lakefront scene.

So, here we are—hunched over the coffee table with the fireplace crackling, piecing together Lake Michigan while we nibble on chips and salsa, fancy cheese, and sliced oranges. Nessa's telling me about the history of Hanukkah. I'd heard about the story where a small amount of oil lasted for seven days and eight nights—it was the answer to a trivia question one night at

McGee's—but I'd never heard about the Maccabees, a group of Jewish rebels who revolted against an evil Greek emperor, winning back the Temple in Jerusalem. Her eyes are sparkling, and I find myself captivated by them, the way her expressions flicker over her face like a movie screen.

"What?" Nessa says, raising an eyebrow as she catches me staring.

I'm just thinking about how pretty you are.

"Nothing." I shake my head. "Just wondering how else to pass the time today."

Truth is, I can think of a few things, but they all require a level of closeness I'm still not sure she's up for. Last night, there were some moments where I thought she was feeling it...and this morning, with those chocolate kisses. But she's pulled back every time I thought she might initiate something, like she's retreating into herself, which gives me even more reason to be cautious about crossing any boundaries. I don't blame her—I wouldn't want to kiss me right now, un-showered and wearing the clothes I slept in.

Nessa glances out the window; it's still snowing but lighter now, the flakes lazily drifting down. "Want to go outside?"

I laugh. "And what, play in the snow like kids?"

"Sure," she says, her smile mischievous. "Unless you're too grown-up for that."

"Never—it's why I'm going into pediatrics." Which is true—working with kids always felt like the perfect fit for me. I love how they see the world, how they can be scared one minute and laughing the next. I love finding creative ways to connect with them, to make the hospital feel like a safe space.

But the hardest part? The part I don't like to talk about, even to myself, is when I can't help them. When a kid is suffering, and I can't fix it. That feeling of helplessness keeps me up at night and makes me question if I'm even cut out for this.

But I'm not going to let my mind go to that dark place right now. I stand, rolling my shoulders like I'm warming them up, and face Nessa. "Prepare yourself, because I'm the reigning snowball champion of Mountain View Elementary."

"Ooh, impressive. Let's see if you've still got it!"

AFTER BUNDLING up in coats and hats, gloves and scarves, we head outside into a world transformed. The usual city sounds are muffled beneath nearly two feet of snow, the air thick with silence. It's like everything has been wrapped in a shimmering, silver blanket, every tree branch outlined in white, every sound swallowed up.

I'm taking it all in when—whack! A snowball smacks me in the back of the head.

I turn to see Nessa grinning like a mischievous little elf from across the snow-covered courtyard, the white pom-pom on her hat bobbing. "What are you waiting for?" she calls. "Show me what you've got!"

"Oh, you're going to regret that." Scooping up a handful of snow, I let it fly...and it soars foot over her head.

"Ha!" she crows. "You throw like a grandpa!"

Before I know it, another snowball flies my way, hitting me square in the chest. I stagger back dramatically, clutching my chest like I've been mortally wounded.

"Yes!" she shouts, fist-pumping.

Laughing, I make another snowball and lob it in her direction, missing again, and she squeals with delight and hits me with another snowball.

But when my third snowball misses her, she narrows her eyes at me suspiciously. "Wait a minute—are you missing on purpose?"

"Me? Never!"

She points a gloved finger at me. "Come on, Jack. Hit me! I dare you!"

35

Grinning, I form a few more snowballs, feeling the competitive spirit kick in. "You asked for it."

I wind up and throw a fastball—aiming it just off her right shoulder—then send another flying inches from her left hip and a final one slamming into the toe of her boot, where I know it won't hurt her.

Her eyes go wide. "Did you play baseball or something?"

"Just one year at a junior college. I'm not that good, but I love it."

She stares at me, something flickering in her eyes. "Ever play football?"

I shake my head, chuckling. "Nope. My mom's a neurologist—she would've disowned me."

"Smart lady."

Then, without warning, she runs toward me, barreling into my stomach with her shoulder and sending us both crashing into a snowdrift. My back hits the snow first, and she lands on top of me, both of us gasping with laughter.

And then everything goes still.

She's close enough that I can see the snowflakes caught on her lashes, the little curls escaping from under her hat. Her cheeks are flushed, her eyes shining, and her lips...

I reach up and cup her face, my gloved thumb brushing along her cheekbone. For a moment, the rest of the world fades away. It's not just that she's beautiful, though she is. It's the way she's breathed life back into me. She's made me laugh, helped me relax, reminded me what it feels like to have fun. Somehow, in less than twenty-four hours, I feel less like an exhausted husk of myself and more like *me.*

Then she glances up, behind me. "The power's back on."

I twist around; sure enough, there's a subtle glow of light from her apartment window. The same window she looked out of when I was smashing up the snowmen.

Feels like a lifetime ago.

"You can charge your phone," she says. "See if you have any alerts from the airline."

Strange, I'd forgotten all about that. "Good idea." Though I don't want to move.

As we head back inside, relief and excitement settle in my chest—hopefully, I can catch a flight home later today. But underneath that, there's another feeling, quieter but impossible to ignore. A flicker of...disappointment?

I glance over at Nessa, snowflakes still caught in her hair, and it hits me like one of her snowballs: if I didn't have somewhere else to be, I'd be just fine staying right here.

CHAPTER 10

December 25, 11:34 am
NESSA

"*L*et there be light!" I call out as I swing my apartment door open. The living room has come back to life—the TV is on, and the *A Christmas Story* marathon is still playing. It's the leg lamp scene, almost the same place it was when the power went out last night.

Jack would get a kick out of that if he were here; he went home to shower and change. I wish he'd hurry back. But then it hits me: what if he *doesn't* come back? His power is back on—maybe he was just hanging out to stay warm, nothing to do with me, personally. A mean little voice sneaks into my mind, whispering the words that nag at me all too often lately: that I'm not enough to be anyone's first choice.

My phone—charging on the kitchen counter—chimes. When I pick it up, I see a bunch of Happy almost-Hanukkah texts and pictures that have come in from my roommates and parents. Julie, from her cruise stop in Key West—a parrot on her shoulder. Amanda, a selfie with her boyfriend snowshoeing by the lake in

Michigan. And my parents on the beach holding margaritas, smiling at each other like no one else exists but them.

I'm thrilled for all of them—but it's a reminder that everyone I love has someone else they love more. At this stage in my life, my friends are pairing off, and my parents are in their second act, and I'm here. Just with myself. And maybe Jack, if he hasn't gotten sick of me yet.

I shake that off—he said he'd be right back, and I have no reason to doubt him. It's just that the apartment feels empty without him. Lonely. I miss him, which is crazy. Because less than twenty-four hours ago, the only thing I knew about the man was that he was probably a doctor, he was definitely a runner, and he had calves that made me weak in the knees.

But in this short window of time, Jack has grown even more attractive to me. Now I know how much humor and heart there is behind his dazzling blue eyes. How smart he is, how he listens and pays attention with his whole body, how much he loves his family. And despite missing them, he's helped make this holiday brighter, even with sub-zero temperatures and no power.

There was a moment out there when I was sure he was going to kiss me—his gloved hand was like ice on my face, and I shivered even as my skin lit up at his touch. But then I had to go and blow it, noticing the electricity was back on. At this rate, the man might not kiss me until New Years Eve. If we're still stranded here together...which wouldn't be so bad.

He's probably finished showering by now, so I should get a move on if I don't want to be a smelly elf when he gets back. Then he'll never want to kiss me.

THIRTY MINUTES LATER, I've showered and shaved (just in case!) and am drying my hair when there's a knock at my door.

"It's open," I call as I walk out of the bathroom. I decided to stay cozy and warm, wearing a fresh pair of leggings, a tank, and an oversized sweater. It's going to take a while for this ancient heating system to get the apartment back to a bearable temperature.

Jack walks in, looking clean and fresh and as excited as—well, a kid on Christmas morning. His arms are full of bags and boxes of frozen food.

"What've you got there?" I ask, leaning against the wall.

"Potatoes," he says. "Hashbrowns, French fries, and mashed."

"I thought you said your fridge was empty?"

"It is." He bumps my shoulder on his way to the kitchen. "But my freezer was stocked. I thought we could maybe use this stuff to make some kind of latke-like objects. I'm sure they won't be as good as the ones you make with your roommates, but it could be fun. And tasty. What do you think?"

My eyes well with tears. What I think is that this is the sweetest, most thoughtful thing anyone has ever done for me, and that Jack is the sweetest, most thoughtful person, and I'm sorry he got stranded in Chicago, but I'm so glad he's here with me. I didn't realize how sad I'd been until he reminded me how it feels to be happy.

But I don't have the words to say all that, so I walk into the kitchen and wrap my arms around him. Jack stiffens at first, as if he doesn't realize what I'm doing—but after a moment, his body seems to melt into mine, and he hugs me back.

"Thank you," I say, squeezing tight.

"It's nothing," he says, but the way he's rubbing my back doesn't feel like nothing. His hands linger there, a slow, deliberate pressure that sends shivers across my skin. His breath brushes against my hair, and the air around us seems to thicken.

My heart picks up, my pulse racing as every nerve in my body becomes aware of how close we are. How easy it would be to tip this into something more.

I pull back slightly, just enough to look up into his eyes. There's a question in them again, like he's waiting for something.

And before I can second-guess myself, I blurt out, "Are you ever going to kiss me?"

Jack's eyebrows lift. "I'm already invading your space; I didn't want...I'm trying to follow your lead."

"But *you* have to lead."

"Why?" he asks, tucking a stray curl behind my ear. That gesture again.

"Because..." I break eye contact and look instead at the stack of frozen food on the counter. I know this is silly, and it's not something I've ever had to actually talk about. Most guys are more than happy to make the first move. It's later they backtrack —I work too much, or I get too excited about things, or I expect too much. I am, overall, too much.

"Hey," Jack says. "You can tell me."

And for some reason, I get the feeling he won't laugh or judge me. That he'll understand and finally just give me what I need, what we both want. I take a deep breath and say, "Because I don't do that."

"Do what?" He slides his hand under my chin and lifts my face toward him, so I have no choice but to look him in the eye. "Kiss?"

"No," I laugh, awkward and too loud. "I love kissing, I *love* it. And I'm really good at it, from what I've been told. I just don't make the first move."

"Ever? Like never?"

"Not since eighth grade. I had a bad experience—misread some signals and ended up embarrassing myself. So ever since then, I just decided I'd let the guy make the first move. Less risk of mortification."

Jack frowns, which was not the response I was going for. "That makes me sad for what you've missed out on."

"Oh, I haven't missed out," I say. "I've kissed *plenty* of people."

"Yeah, but you're missing out on that thrill of vulnerability when you decide to put yourself out there. That pulse racing moment when you lean in, how time seems to slow down and every second feels like a minute until the other person leans in, too, tilts their head…"

Without meaning to, I tilt my head as he says the words—then snap out of it. I step back, my heart thudding against my ribcage. It's too hard to think about this, to talk about it when his hands are on me, creating sparks with his touch.

"Yeah, well, maybe you've never put yourself out there, being all vulnerable only to get rejected. To be laughed at, to feel like you've thrown yourself off a cliff and there was no one there to catch you."

Jack's expression softens, a flicker of understanding in his eyes. "I've felt that plenty of times. But…"

"But what?" I challenge, my voice sharper than I mean it to be. I just want him to *kiss* me.

"But it's like you said about the Christmas music. The risk is worth it, especially when the reward can be so incredibly sweet. There's nothing to be scared of."

"I'm not scared," I say, even though a part of me is. The fourteen-year-old girl I used to be—the one who couldn't trust her instincts, who built walls to avoid getting hurt.

"Then kiss me."

His words hang in the air between us, my heart once again pounding so loudly I'm sure he can hear it. Everything in me wants to close the gap, to let myself fall into this moment—but then I shake my head. "This is ridiculous!"

Jack is looking at me with an expression somewhere between curious and compassionate, and something shifts. Maybe I can trust him. Maybe I can trust *this*.

"A kiss is four times more exciting if you're the one initiating it," he says, his eyes dancing with amusement.

"Did you learn that at trivia, too?"

He shrugs, his lips twitching like he's trying not to laugh. His restraint and his so-called respect are as endearing as it is maddening.

I put my hands on my hips. "Are you really going to make me do this?"

"I'm not going to make you do anything." He's smirking at me, eyes glinting with challenge as he leans against the counter and folds his arms. "But I hope you will—or we can always start defrosting these potatoes and..."

Oh, fuck it.

Before he can finish his sentence, I close the distance between us. I reach my hand up behind his neck and bring his head down as I tilt mine up toward his. Our lips brush—once, twice—and I feel it: the thrill, the vulnerability, the electricity.

I pull back an inch and lift my eyes to his, taking a shaky breath.

"Good job," he whispers.

I nod, proud of myself but also a little disappointed it's already over. But then Jack cups my face in his hand and pulls my mouth to his again.

He immediately parts my lips with an urgency that steals my breath. It's not just a kiss; it's a pull, a dive, dragging us deeper and deeper. When our tongues meet, it's like a spark lighting a fuse—warmth blooms in my chest, making my pulse race, and all I can do is hold on.

When his hands slide to the nape of my neck, his fingers tangling in my hair, I let out a low moan and clutch his flannel shirt, pulling him closer, needing more of him. His mouth shifts to my jaw, then my throat, and my head rolls back as I give in to the sensation. It's all-consuming, a soul-bending kiss that makes me forget time, space, anything that isn't him. It's just us, floating in some in-between place where nothing matters but the sweetness of his mouth, the soft sounds of pleasure rumbling in his throat, the warmth of his breath fanning against my skin.

All too soon, his kisses become softer, gentler, feather-light until he pulls back, leaving me with one last lingering kiss that keeps me tethered to him, even when it's over.

When I lift my eyes to meet his, he's smiling, his eyes sparkling like the first snowflakes of a storm, catching the light and making everything feel still and quiet. I want to hold onto this feeling, the two of us in this perfect little snow globe of a moment together.

I'm about to lean in to see if the second kiss can be even better than the first when a shrill noise sounds, like an alarm. I flinch, hoping I'm not about to wake up and discover this is all some fever dream.

The sound chimes again, and Jack lets out a disappointed sigh that captures exactly how I feel. He fishes in his pocket and pulls out his phone—I see the word MOMMA🤍 on the screen with an incoming FaceTime call.

"Go ahead," I tell him. "It's okay."

"Thank you." Jack gives me a quick kiss before answering his phone. "Hey, Mom. I miss you guys, too."

CHAPTER 11

December 25, 12:43 pm

JACK

"*Y*ou're with a *girl?*"

On my phone screen, my mom's face is lit up like she's won the lottery. She's decked out in the sequined red hat she wears every Christmas, looking like a younger, fashionable Mrs. Claus.

"What girl?" My dad's face looms into the picture, his mustache quivering with excitement.

I've retreated to the far end of the hallway outside Nessa's apartment, hoping she hasn't overheard any of that. It's not that I meant to tell my parents about her but...well, let's just say that after what just happened in Nessa's kitchen, I'm not exactly *calm, cool, and collected.* My mom picked up on it in about two seconds flat.

Even now, my head is still fuzzy.

"Who's with a girl?" My older sister's voice comes from somewhere off-screen, and I refocus.

Mom squeals. "Jacky!"

"They're snowed in together," Dad tells my sister, waggling his eyebrows.

"And they kissed!" Mom adds, somehow gathering this even though I didn't share the details. How does she do that?

"Ew, poor girl," my sister says.

I roll my eyes. "She's not a girl, she's a woman. And thanks, Nic. Appreciate the support."

"Oh, hush," Mom says over her shoulder. Then she's back to me, her blue eyes softening. "I'm so glad you're not alone. I was worried when we couldn't reach you."

"Only because my phone died," I tell her for the third time. "Sorry for worrying you."

"When's Uncle Jack coming?" a tiny voice in the background pipes up—my six-year-old niece, Gabrielle.

Then I hear my three-year-old nephew Sammy chanting, "Unca-Jack! Unca-Jack!"

"He'll get here as soon as he can, guys," a deeper voice says. My brother-in-law, Eddie.

A lump rises in my throat. They're all gathered together, everyone in holiday mode. I can hear Frank Sinatra crooning in the background, can practically smell the cinnamon rolls, and hear the crinkle of wrapping paper.

"There's room on a flight leaving at 6 p.m. tonight," Dad says. "I'm looking right now. Should I buy you a ticket?"

"Oh, you don't have—"

"Of course we do!" Mom interjects, but then she glances at my dad, and something passes unspoken between them. She glances back at me. "Listen, sweetheart, we know you're exhausted—if it's too much to come here, if you'd rather use the time to catch up on sleep, we understand."

"We'd love to have you come home," Dad adds.

"But do what's best for *you*, okay?" Mom finishes.

My parents crowd together, cheek to cheek, smiling expectantly as they wait for my response.

And I want to say yes. I want to be home. I want to sit at our kitchen table, my mom handing me a cup of coffee, my dad clapping a hand on my shoulder, and finally let everything spill out—the stress, the second-guessing, the nagging fear that coming here for residency and maybe even pursuing medicine at all, was a huge mistake. And worst of all, the fact that I'm struggling so much when all residents go through the same stuff. It's not like I'm special; we all work long hours, we all see tragedy. So what's wrong with *me*? Why can't I handle it? I've kept all this bottled up for months, trying to sound upbeat on our calls so my parents wouldn't worry. Going home is my chance to leave all that behind for a few days. To reset so I can figure out how to keep going.

But then I think of Nessa, back in that apartment, her eyes going all teary with gratitude when I offered to help make latkes —which is nothing compared to everything she's done for me.

If I get on a flight at 6 pm, I won't be here at sundown. I hate the thought of leaving her alone on the first night of Hanukkah, especially after everything she did to make Christmas morning special.

Not to mention: that *kiss*.

And the fact that I want to do it again.

"What about tomorrow morning?" I hear myself say.

My mom's smile fades slightly, but Dad grins, his eyes twinkling in a knowing way. "Got it. Tomorrow it is—I'll text you the details."

WHEN I WALK BACK into Nessa's apartment, she's standing by the kitchen counter, a jar of peanut butter in her hands. She's brought out a menorah, too, gold and gleaming, with a few candles on the table next to it.

She looks up as I enter, her expression cautious, like she's bracing herself. The memory of our kiss hits me like a wave, filling my head with the softness of her lips, the warmth of her hands sliding up my back.

"Everything okay?" she asks.

I clear my throat, trying to get a grip. "Yeah, my parents were checking in about getting me a flight home tonight."

And just like that, Nessa's light dims and her big brown eyes flash with disappointment. Almost immediately, she summons up a smile, then turns back to the sandwich she's making.

"And you did?" Her voice is light, casual. "That's…that's great, Jack. I'm so happy for you."

I walk over, stopping a foot behind her. My eyes drift down her body, conjuring up a memory of how it felt to hold her, to run my hands down those curves. Somehow, she's made a ponytail, sweater, and leggings look unbelievably gorgeous. I'm close enough to feel the warmth radiating off her, close enough that her scent—something soft and floral—blurs my thoughts.

"Actually," I say, "there weren't any flights tonight. The airport's still closed."

Her head lifts. "Oh?"

Something in her voice—vulnerability; hope—makes me take another step forward.

Slowly, I slide my arms around her from behind, pulling her toward me until her back is pressed to my chest. She inhales sharply but doesn't pull away. Instead, she curves against me, her body softening as she leans into me.

I lower my mouth, pressing a soft, lingering kiss to the curve of her neck. She shivers, her pulse fluttering under my lips. I kiss her again, my mouth trailing up to her jaw, and she tilts her head, inviting me to explore. I'm happy to oblige, deepening the kisses as my hands span her waist, slide down to her hips, pulling her against me harder. Her breath hitches. If she had any question about how I'm feeling about her—I'm pretty sure that cleared it up.

When my teeth lightly scrape her earlobe, she lets out a quiet moan and grips the counter to steady herself. For a split second, I wonder what it would take to convince her to completely let go— to let herself feel everything she's been holding back.

But for now, I stay right here, kissing her warm skin, savoring every taste, every sound she makes, as if there's nothing beyond this moment.

"Looks like you're stuck with me for another night," I murmur. "As long as you're okay with that?"

Her voice is a whisper, barely audible: "I think I can probably make the best of it."

CHAPTER 12

December 25, 1:37 pm
NESSA

*J*ack is staying another night! Of course, I'm sorry he can't get home to his family, but I'm thrilled he'll be staying here with me.

Also: *damn* is he a good kisser. I don't know if it was the buildup of all that tension or the fact that I initiated it, or because it was Jack I was kissing—but he was right, it was at least four times better than any other kiss I've ever had.

We're still in the kitchen, eating peanut butter and brown sugar sandwiches (my dad's specialty that I loved as a kid) while we try to figure out how we're going to make latkes with the ingredients he foraged from his freezer.

"Do you really eat these?" I ask, holding up one of the Hungry Man frozen dinners. The Salisbury steak and green beans won't be of use, but the side of "homestyle" mashed potatoes will be clutch.

He nods. "Sometimes I'm barely home long enough to eat and

shower, then crash for a few hours before waking up and heading back to the hospital. They do the trick."

"That's sad."

He shrugs, grimacing. "That's my life right now. Sad."

Something about his expression tugs at me. It reminds me of the way he looked when he first walked into my place last night —defeated. I'd assumed it was just because he missed his flight, but maybe there's more to it.

"Really?" I say, concerned. "You're not enjoying being a resident?"

He huffs, shaking his head. "It's not meant to be *enjoyable.* It's meant to teach you a lot of information and give you a ton of experience, crammed into a few brutal years, all while being pushed to your limit so you're prepared for whatever happens and can be the best doctor possible."

His voice sounds hollow, like he's reciting a script, one he's heard—or told himself—too many times.

"But hopefully it'll be worth it?" I offer, not knowing what else to say.

He hesitates, his shoulders sagging. "I mean, I knew it would be hard, but it's… more than I expected. Some days, I wonder if I'm cut out for it."

The confession hangs between us, honest and raw. He runs a hand through his hair, avoiding my gaze. "Like yesterday, a teenage girl came in with meningitis and died three hours later— we ran the code, did chest compressions, the whole thing. Her mom and grandmother were there watching it all happen and…" He shakes his head, his eyes going glassy, like he's back in that hospital room.

"And last week," he goes on, "I had the cutest little four-year-old with leukemia. Doing well with treatment, but then he catches pneumonia and he's just…gone. And his parents—"

Jack's voice catches. He blinks hard and clears his throat. "It's starting to feel like no matter what I do, no matter how hard I try to help them, it doesn't matter."

His eyes meet mine, his expression guarded, like he's waiting for judgment. I want to reach out, take his hand, somehow help him see what I can see so clearly: that he cares deeply about these patients and their families, that he would do anything for them.

"It sounds like you're doing the best you can," I say, knowing it probably sounds trite.

"Maybe my best isn't good enough."

"Jack..." I whisper, my heart aching for him. I know that feeling—the nagging worry of not being enough. I want to tell him that, but before I can, he blinks and gives me a lopsided, apologetic smile.

"Sorry. First time I've really said any of that out loud." He clears his throat and turns his attention back to the frozen dinner. "Anyway, did you know that Salisbury steak was invented by Dr. James Salisbury during the Civil War to help soldiers digest their food more easily?"

I shake my head, a smile tugging at the corners of my lips. "I did not. Is it even steak?"

"It is not," Jack admits, laughing, back to the guy I've gotten to know in the past few hours. "But it comes with potatoes, which is the point—right?"

"Right." But in my head, I'm already doubling my Sunday meal prep for the week, making enough for Jack so he doesn't have to eat these frozen sodium bombs. So he has a little bit of comfort to look forward to after a long day at the hospital taking care of everyone else.

Slow down, Nessa, I scold myself. The last thing I want is to scare Jack away by going way overboard and doing too much—my usual MO. I should just focus on the here and now, making the best of the situation we're in. Making lemonade out of lemons. Or, in this case, latkes out of frozen potatoes.

. . .

AN HOUR AND A HALF LATER, we're sitting on the couch about to dig into our latke-like objects and watch Jack's favorite Christmas movie, which is apparently controversial.

"What do we think?" Jack asks, looking down at the plate of fried potato goodness in front of us.

"Well, they look like latkes—but the real measure will be in how they taste."

We put the ingredients Jack brought into ChatGPT, and it spit out a recipe for us: equal parts mashed potatoes, finely chopped French fries, and pre-cooked hash browns, plus a few other things we had in the apartment—eggs, flour, salt and pepper. And of course, the condiments.

"Which do you recommend?" Jack asks, nodding toward the two bowls I put on the table.

"That depends what team you're on."

Jack quirks an eyebrow.

"You see, there are a lot of different kinds of Jews. You may have heard of some of them—like Sephardic or Ashkenazi. Orthodox, Conservative, or Reform. But..." I pause for effect. "The one thing that really divides us is the question: do you put sour cream or applesauce on your latkes."

Jack nods as if he's filing the information away for a future trivia contest. "I should probably try them both."

"Good decision."

I watch as he cuts a latke in half and puts one of the toppings on each piece. He's taking this seriously, and I both appreciate it and find it hilarious.

"Gotta cleanse my palate," he says, taking a big sip of water and swirling it around his mouth.

The sour cream one is first. "Crunchy, creamy, tart."

Another sip of water. Then, the applesauce. "Sweet, but not too sweet."

"So?" I ask. He kept his expression stoic, so I couldn't tell which one he liked better.

"I didn't dislike either of them," he says. "But if I had to choose one…." He takes another bite of each. "I'd have to say I'm an Applesauce Gentile. The sweet and salty just does it for me."

"I knew I liked you." I heap a spoonful of applesauce and an extra dash of salt on my own latke. "Now let's get into the Christmas spirit by watching Bruce Willis try to stop some bad guys—which sounds oddly Jewish. Most of our holiday stories involve a tragedy and how we persevered."

I tell him abridged stories of several Jewish holidays—including Passover and our escape from slavery in Egypt, and Purim, where an evil man was stopped from annihilating the Jews in Persia—and by the time I finish, he's staring at me, mouth open.

My cheeks flush. "Sorry, that was a lot. Sometimes I get excited and don't know when to stop."

"No, I love it." He taps his temple. "Can never have too many factoids stored up here to bust out."

I laugh, relieved.

"And never apologize for getting excited," he says, knocking his shoulder into mine. "It's cute."

My cheeks flush again—this time, from pleasure. His words can't erase all the times I've been told I'm "too much," but they nudge some of the ache aside. For the first time, I wonder if someone might see my quirks, my enthusiasm, everything I've tried to tone down—and think I'm just right.

"You know who else is cute?" I say, and Jack's eyebrows do a little dance. "Yes, you. Obviously. But I was thinking about Bruce Willis."

Jack laughs and throws his arm around my shoulder. I'm thrilled—until he grabs the remote and hits play. Apparently, he actually wants to watch the movie.

Oh well. I snuggle into his side and pull the blankets up around us. We can Netflix now, then do the "and chill" part after.

Something to look forward to…

CHAPTER 13

December 25, 4:46 pm
JACK

"So, my first night of Hannukah," I say, glancing at Nessa with a grin. "What do I need to know?"

Somehow, I made it through an entire movie with my arm around Nessa, my body hyperaware of every sound and movement she made. Now it's just after sundown, and we're standing side by side at the kitchen table, where the menorah is sitting on top of a sheet of aluminum foil—to catch any dripping wax, she explained. Her menorah is more elaborate than the ones I've seen before—one tall candle holder in the middle with four on each side, all of it adorned with silver leaves and flowers. Two slender candles are already set in place, one in the middle and one in the far-right spot.

Nessa gestures to the middle candle. "This one's called the shamash, the helper candle. We'll use it to light the other one. But first, we say a blessing."

She strikes a match, the scent of sulfur sparking in the air, and

I lean in, my eyes fixed on her face as she carefully lights the shamash.

"What's the blessing?" I ask, my voice low, not wanting to break the spell.

She grins, a little shy, and glances down. "If you want to try, you can repeat after me."

There's a sweetness to her, a sort of quiet pride in sharing this with me, that makes me want to be as present as possible. Her face glows in the candlelight, her expression softened by the flickering flame, and I can't help thinking about how much I want to pull her close again.

But I hold myself back. Because as much as I want her—and I think she wants me, too—I want more. I want to know what it's like to take her out on a date, to listen to her talk about a busy day at work, to make her laugh over a morning coffee. I want her to know that this—whatever it is between us—isn't just about the attraction, even though that's definitely part of it. I don't want her to think I'm only here because of the storm or the flight delays.

Those may have brought me here, but she's the reason I'm staying.

She begins the blessing in Hebrew, *"Baruch atah Adonai..."* her voice soft but steady, and I repeat the words after her with every new phrase she speaks, stumbling a bit over the pronunciation.

"...shel Hanukkah."

"Shel Hannukah," I repeat.

"Not bad for a beginner," she teases, her eyes shining as she looks up at me.

I grin. "Well, you're a good teacher."

She offers the lit shamash to me. "You can do the honors."

Our fingers brush as I take the candle, and somehow—even though we spent hours tangled up together watching the movie—that small touch sends a spark through me. I hope this means something to her, too. Not just the ritual, but me being here with her, taking part in it.

Her hand slides over mine, guiding me to light the first night's candle, and as it catches, the glow between us brightens. There's something almost sacred in the quiet, a stillness that feels like it belongs just to us.

"What now?" I ask, keeping my voice low

"The candles have to burn for at least thirty minutes, but it's tradition to let them burn all the way down."

"And you do this every night?"

Nessa nods. "Each night, we add another candle to the menorah going from right to left—but we light them from left to right."

"Huh," I say, taking it all in. I had no idea how much I didn't know about this holiday. It feels important to remember, just in case this Hanukkah won't be our last. "Do you still start with the sha…"

"The shamash—that's always first. But then we light the newest candle next. I think it has something to do with honoring the present moment—the here and now—before lighting the previous ones. A reminder to live in the present and celebrate each day's progress, not just focus on the past. And every night, the light grows until it fills the whole menorah. Because the more light we give, the more we have to share."

"I love that." And I'd love to believe that the more I give, the more I have to share. But right now, all I can think about is how little I have left. The long hours, the death and grief—it's all piling up. I don't know how much light is left in me.

Refocusing, I smile at Nessa. "I'm really glad I'm here tonight. Thank you for sharing this with me."

"Thank you for letting me share it—it forced me to actually think about what it all means instead of going through the motions. As a kid, I wanted to get through the boring stuff so we could open presents and play dreidel."

I chuckle, imagining a tiny version of Nessa, her hair a halo of dark curls. "I was like that when we did Advent, growing up. We'd sit around the kitchen table, just me, my sister, and my parents, and read parts of the Christmas story while the candles burned. I was kind of a pain in the ass about it as a teenager."

Nessa grins, curiosity sparking in her eyes. "What did you do?"

"Oh, I'd drop 'fun facts' about how the Christmas story probably didn't actually happen that way, or how the Gospels weren't even written until decades later." I shake my head, the guilt still faintly lingering.

She tilts her head. "So what is Advent, exactly? I know about the calendar with chocolate, but that's it."

I lean forward, surprised at how excited I am to tell her—like it's my small way of thanking her for sharing all this with me. "It's a weekly countdown to Christmas. There are four candles in a wreath and one in the center. Each candle represents something —hope, peace, joy, love—and we light one each Sunday in December. Then we light the center candle on Christmas Eve. We stopped doing it when I went to college, but my mom started again this year with my niece and nephew…"

Her face softens. "And you missed it."

I nod, feeling that familiar ache in my chest. Before I can say anything more, she stands and goes into the living room, then returns holding a few of the candles we were burning earlier.

She sets four in a circle on the table and one in the middle. "I don't have a wreath, but kind of like this?"

A lump rises unexpectedly in my throat, and I swallow. "Yeah. That's it."

She hands me the matchbox and I pull one out, then hesitate, remembering how she offered me the shamash, how it felt when she invited me to join something that matters to her.

"Would you do the honors?" I say.

Her lips curve in a pleased smile. "Sure."

She lights each candle, and as the light grows, warmth settles on my shoulders. For a moment, it's almost like my family is here with me.

"So, what did your mom say," Nessa says, nudging me. "When you were being a pain-in-the-ass teenager about Advent?"

I grin. "She'd say I was missing the point. That the point of the Christmas story isn't all the details but the meaning behind it. She told me I needed to focus on the message."

"And what's the message?"

Shaking my head, I chuckle. "I asked her the same thing. She said I needed to figure it out myself."

"Classic mom move," she says, laughing.

"Yeah," I say fondly. "She's the best."

Nessa smiles, her eyes softening. "That makes me think of my Bubbe—every year, she would remind us that Hanukkah wasn't about the presents, but the miracle of it all. She said the lesson was learning to trust that there will be enough. That even when things look impossible, what we've been given and what we have to offer is enough."

Her words settle over me, heavy and comforting all at once. I think back to everything I told her earlier today about how I'm feeling—the children facing battles they never should've had to fight, families breaking under the weight—and how she said I'm doing the best I can.

I've spent so much time questioning whether I can make a difference, doubting if my efforts are worth it. But for the first time, I consider that maybe it's not about fixing everything. It's about showing up. Giving what I can. And trusting that, in the end, it'll be enough.

"Thanks for sharing that," I say, watching the lights flickering between us—the candles on Nessa's beautiful menorah plus the mismatched Advent wreath she made for me, just so I could have a little taste of home. "Interesting how candles are important in both holidays."

"Finding light in the darkness," she says. "Hope even in the worst of times."

"Like, a baby born in a barn can grow up to change the world."

"And a tiny bit of oil," she says softly, "can burn for seven days and eight nights."

"Or getting stranded in a snowstorm with a stranger and finding a friend."

"And maybe..." Nessa swallows, her lashes lowering as she looks down. "More than a friend."

Her eyes meet mine and everything goes quiet, as if the entire world is taking a deep breath. My gaze drifts down to her lips, watching as they part slightly, catching the pink tip of her tongue as she wets her bottom lip.

A wave of heat rolls through me, making my fingers twitch with the urge to touch her. It's not just attraction—though that's undeniable—it's this *pull* between us. This unexpected connection that's deepening with every word, every glance.

I clear my throat. "So...now what do we do?"

"Well, like I said, we'd usually play dreidel," she says, grinning. "It's a kids' game, though."

"Sounds fun," I say genuinely. A kids' game feels like exactly what I need right now.

But then she raises an eyebrow, a mischievous smile tugging at her lips. "Unless...we make it a little more grown-up."

"What do you have in mind?"

Her eyes sparkle. "How would you feel about *strip* dreidel?"

CHAPTER 14

December 25, 5:55 pm
NESSA

*W*hat has gotten into me? Maybe it's the holiday spirit or the fact that we're on day two of being snowed in. Or maybe, probably, most likely, it's Jack.

He's in the living room now, waiting while I go in my bedroom to get the dreidel and the chocolate gelt my mom sent, along with a couple of presents. And a few other items he isn't expecting...

"What did you do?" Jack asks when I turn the corner, a giant grin on his face.

"I don't know what you're talking about?" I hold my hands out at my side, in part because I can't lower them.

"Were you cold?" He nods toward the extra layers I added to my outfit—two more sweaters, a scarf, and a hat.

"If anything, I'm a little warm," I admit, sitting on the couch beside him. "But it gives me a better chance of winning."

"Ahhh."

"Except it really is hot in here now." I unwrap the scarf from around my neck and then peel off one of the sweaters. "It's what we did when we played in college. But back then, we didn't want to lose all our clothes."

Jack's eyebrows shoot up at the implication. I'd usually be embarrassed by my accidental admission, but by this point, it's not a secret that I want to pick up where we left off earlier.

But first, we have a game to play.

"Okay," I say, laying everything on the coffee table. "Have you ever played before?"

Jack shakes his head, so I divide out the chocolate coins and teach him how to spin the dreidel, holding the tip between his thumb and middle finger and making almost a snapping movement.

"Like this?" he asks, literally snapping. The dreidel topples.

"No, like this." I take the dreidel and spin, sending it dancing down the length of the table, where it stops and twirls like a ballerina until it falls.

Jack tries again, and again, it falls.

"You'll get the hang of it," I say. "And if not, it might be a quick game."

I explain the rest of the rules, showing him how each side of the plastic dreidel has a different Hebrew letter written on it. If the dreidel lands on a Nun, nothing happens. If he gets a Gimmel, he takes all the coins in the pot. For a Hey, he gets half of the coins, and with Shin, he has to put one in.

"And where does the stripping come in?" Jack asks.

"Well, in college, we took off a piece of clothing whenever we ran out of gelt—but that might take all night with just two of us."

His eyes glint. "I have an idea."

"We skip the game and take off all our clothes?" My heart flutters in my chest.

"Come on, where's the fun in that?" He pauses, smirking. "I mean, there's plenty of fun in that—but this is Hanukkah. This night should be different than all other nights, right?"

"Wrong holiday—that's Passover."

Jack brushes a loose strand of hair behind my ear, sending a shiver down my spine. "Well, this is my first Hanukkah, and I want to play strip dreidel."

"Okay," I say. "Tell me your idea."

My face is flushed from a combination of the fire in the fireplace, the two sweaters I'm wearing, and the man beside me, his leg pressed against mine. I slip my last extra sweater off and toss it on the floor—I don't want to add any additional barriers to getting what I think we both want tonight.

"What's the letter where you get all the coins again?" Jack asks.

"Gimmel."

"Okay, so when you get Gimmel, you win the coins, and the other person loses a piece of clothing."

"And the winner gets to take it off the loser," I add, upping the stakes. He agrees, and I'm not sure if I'm more excited about the idea of taking off his clothes or having him take off mine.

"Let the game begin," Jack says, his eyes locking with mine. The flicker of candlelight dances between us, the fire crackles softly, casting shadows that make his face look angular. A little dangerous. He nudges the dreidel toward me. "Ladies first."

His voice—a little raspy—scrapes something deep inside me. My first spin, I get a Gimmel and take all the coins from the pot, then look up to see Jack watching me, a speculative gleam in his eyes.

"You get to choose what I take off," I remind him. *Please pick your shirt.*

He quirks an eyebrow, fingers sliding up to graze the collar of his flannel. I bite my lip, anticipation thrumming in my veins— but then he scoots back on the couch and lifts his left leg on my lap. "You can de-sock me."

"Such a tease." I slip my hands up the leg of his jeans, my fingers brushing his skin, calling to mind all the times I stared at his calves. Slowly, I slide my fingers under the top edge of the sock and pull it off, tossing it in the pile along with my discarded sweaters. "Your turn."

It takes Jack three attempts to get the dreidel to spin, and when it does, it lands on Shin.

"Put a coin in," I tell him, just a little smug.

I land on another Gimmel, take the pot, and slip off Jack's left sock.

We hit an unlucky streak: Hey. Hey. Nun. Shin. And then Jack finally lands on a Gimmel. He looks up, smirking as he takes the coins. "What do you want me to take off?"

I could pick a sock, too. Or I could up the ante. Heart pounding, I lick my lips before saying, "My sweater."

His eyes flash with heat. "Gladly."

I shift my torso toward him, giving him better access. Holding my gaze, he slowly lifts the sweater up, maintaining eye contact until I disappear beneath it. His fingers brush a sliver of exposed skin near my waist, and my skin prickles into goosebumps.

When I reappear, Jack tosses my sweater on the pile, looking a tiny bit disappointed that I have a tank top underneath. His eyes linger on my neckline, drifting down my body as his lips part, and I'm about to suggest we forget the rest of the game and get moving.

Then he sits back, running his hands through his hair like he's trying to pull himself together. "Your spin."

We each land on Shin, throwing a coin into the pot. Then he gets a Hey, taking half the coins, before I finally land on another Gimmel.

"Well, that's a shame." He flashes me a devious grin. "I guess you better take this off."

He motions to his flannel shirt. I take my time undoing each button, and now I'm the one who's disappointed when I realize he's wearing an undershirt. Damn these winter layers! It's been months since I first saw him coming back from a run, and I want to see if his chest is as glorious as I remember it.

As luck would have it, my next spin is a Gimmel. "Sorry for your loss," I say, smiling.

His eyes darken as he looks at me. "I'm not."

I take my time, lifting his cotton undershirt inch by inch, my hands skimming his warm, soft skin as I go. He releases a shaky breath.

"Wow," I breathe as he comes into view. He's beautiful, broad and lean, his skin flickering as the candlelight dances across it. I bring a hand to his chest, then hesitate. He nods permission.

I exhale a sigh and lay my palm flat on his chest, running it over his smooth skin, the firm muscles of his chest and down his belly. His breathing quickens, his body tensing under my touch. Heat rushes through me, settling low between my legs. My hand has a mind of its own and drifts down to the bulge in his pants, my fingers tracing the shape of him, then reach for the fly of his jeans.

"You need a Gimmel first," Jack says, his voice low and husky. "And it's my spin."

I let out a tiny growl of frustration, but nod and put my hand back in my own lap.

While Jack's technique has improved—he can get a solid spin now—his luck has not. We go back and forth: he hits three Shins, losing almost all his gelt to the pot, while I get two Heys and, finally—a Gimmel, taking them all.

Jack doesn't hesitate. He gets off the couch and stands in front of me. *This is it*, I realize as I look up at him, past the smooth contours of his chest and his incredibly broad shoulders. *We're doing this*. His blue eyes are dark with desire, his brown hair mussed from running his hands through it. My own body is a tight knot of lust. I'm desperate to see what he looks like when he loses control—and to be the one responsible for it.

"Happy Hanukkah," I whisper to myself, my fingers fumbling

to unbutton his pants. I slide them down, and Jack kicks them the rest of the way until he's standing before me in boxer briefs covered in reindeer.

I flutter my fingers over the boxers and glance up, asking for permission to reach inside, but Jack shakes his head and grumbles, "Hand me the dreidel."

"But…" I'm prepared to give this man the blow job of his life, and he wants to finish the stupid game?

"Dreidel," he says, almost a command.

I hand him the plastic toy, and he pretends to spin it through the air, holding onto the stem and placing it very deliberately on the table, Gimmel side up.

He doesn't bother with the coins; just reaches down and pulls me up so I'm standing in front of him. "May I?"

I nod, and Jack reaches for my tank top. Despite the rush we're both in, he takes his time, sliding it up and over my head.

His breath hitches when he sees me in the black lace bra I put on earlier in hopes we'd end up right here. Then, even though it's technically my turn now, Jack picks up the dreidel and pretends to spin it on his palm before holding it up for me to see.

"Gimmel," he says. I arch my back, drawing Jack's eyes toward my chest. He bites his lower lip and brings his hands up, cupping my breasts, feeling their fullness before sliding his hands around to the clasp of my bra. He teases at it for an excruciatingly long moment before dropping his hands to my waist.

I let out a huff of disappointment, but then he slips his fingers under the waistband of my leggings. Heat travels up my legs, and my breath grows ragged as he lowers them carefully, like he's unwrapping a present.

When the leggings are off, and we're both in nothing but our underwear, Jack looks up at me, hunger in his eyes.

"Now what?" he asks.

CHAPTER 15

December 25, 6:53 pm
JACK

"That depends on what you want," Nessa says.

She's standing in front of me, looking mouth-wateringly delicious, completely bare except for a black lace bra and matching panties—scratch that; a matching black lace *thong*, I realize as I sneak a quick look over her shoulder at her backside.

"It's not obvious what *I* want?" I glance down at myself; I'm so hard I could probably dent a tin can.

All through the game, I tried to remind myself that I'm not going to rush this, that I want more than one night together. But I'm now finding it impossible to even remember why. Very little blood supply to my brain at the moment.

Not that I'm complaining—it's crystal clear Nessa wants me as much as I want her. She reaches out a finger and trails it down the bulge in my boxers like she did before, but now I'm so sensitive my hips jerk involuntarily. Somehow, I'm on the verge of coming and I haven't even touched her yet.

Copying her movement, I reach out with one finger and

trace down one bra strap, across the cup of her bra, then let my finger dip into her cleavage. Goosebumps spread across her skin, and she sucks in a shaky breath. Then I hook my finger around the tiny bow in the center of her bra and tug her toward me.

In response, she hooks a finger inside the waistband of my boxers and gives me a little tug closer. Now we're inches apart, her chin tilted up to meet my eyes, her pupils dilated and her cheeks pink.

"Your move," I say in a rough voice, and she nods. We both seem to have agreed that we're playing a new game now.

Slowly, she slides her hand inside my boxers and wraps it around me, heat and softness and a sharp wave of pleasure. My heart pounds. I'm aching with the effort of holding back. *Keep it together*, I order myself. *Do not fuck this up.*

It's my move now, so I slide my hands up her ribcage to cup her breasts, feeling her nipples harden as my thumbs drift over the lacy cups of her bra.

She lets out a low moan that somehow makes me even harder, and I lean down and kiss her, rough and urgent, letting my hands roam where they've been wanting to go, sliding them down to her ass, up into her hair, kissing her deeper and deeper until her breaths are quick and shallow and desperate.

"My turn," she says, pulling away.

And before I even have a chance to think, she's kneeling at my feet and sliding down my boxers just enough so she can take me in her mouth.

"Jesus," I hiss.

"Nope, just me."

I half-groan, half-laugh as she takes me deeper, working me with her lips and tongue and hand, warm and slick and perfect. I'm too close to the edge, though—and I'll be damned if I let myself reach the finish line before she does.

So I reach down and lift her chin with my fingers, tugging my boxers back into place with my other hand. "Come here," I murmur.

She stands, and I take her face in my hands. Her eyes are bright, her lips wet, and before I can stop myself, the words tumble out: "You are so damn gorgeous."

She gives a shy smile. "So are you. I've thought so ever since the first time I saw you, coming in from a run. And the second time, waiting for the bus. And the third time…"

My eyebrows lift. "Why didn't you say anything? I would've been *thrilled*."

She shrugs, and her eyes—those big, brown, expressive eyes—flash with a hint of vulnerability. It reminds me of our conversation earlier, about how she doesn't like to make the first move. She's already been so brave tonight. If anyone should initiate the vulnerable conversation before we move forward, it's me.

"Here's the thing, Nessa," I say, doing my best to keep my voice steady. "I'm not a one-night stand kind of guy."

Her eyes snap back to mine, wide and surprised. "Why does this have to be one night?"

"That's what I'm trying to say." I take a breath. "If we do this, you have to promise me you'll let me take you on a proper first date."

"First date?" she repeats, incredulous.

Heat creeps up the back of my neck. "Not if you don't want—"

"Jack," she cuts me off, giving me a mock-disappointed shake of her head. "This is at least our fourth date right now."

I blink, caught off guard. "Fourth?"

"Last night, eating Thai food by the fire? That was our first date," she says, a playful lilt in her voice. "And this morning, opening stockings and then playing outside in the snow? Second date."

A grin spreads across my face as I nod, catching on. "Third date: making latkes and watching the movie."

"Fourth date: lighting the menorah and playing strip dreidel."

She smiles up at me, a glint in her eye. "See? We're totally ready for this."

"Well, when you put it that way…" I duck down and scoop her over my shoulder, making her squeal in surprise.

"Jack!" she yelps as I lift her.

"Where's your bedroom?" I take off toward the hallway.

She kicks her legs, laughing breathlessly. "Second door on the left. But if you drop me—"

"Drop you?" I give her butt a playful smack. "Not a chance. You think I'd break the best present I've gotten this year?"

Her laugh softens into something sweeter as I duck through the doorway, careful not to jostle her. The city lights outside filter through the curtains, painting the room in gold and silver, and I set her down on the bed with exaggerated care.

Nessa looks up at me, her cheeks flushed, her smile glowing. "You always handle your presents this carefully?"

I grin, crawling over her. "Only my favorite one."

Her breath catches, and I swear I see the hint of tears in her eyes.

"What is it?" I ask, concerned.

She hesitates, then gives a self-conscious shrug. "It's just…I don't think I've ever been anyone's favorite."

Something tugs in my chest, fierce and protective. I brush a strand of hair from her face, my thumb lingering on her cheek, searching for the right words to help her understand that this moment, this connection between us, feels special. Unlike anything I've felt before. "You're the gift I didn't know I was wishing for."

Her smile widens, eyes lighting up. "Then maybe you should finish unwrapping."

"Merry Christmas to me," I murmur before capturing her lips with mine.

CHAPTER 16

December 25, 7:11 pm
NESSA

*N*ever did I ever imagine this: Jack, nearly naked in my bedroom, kissing me like I'm just what he asked Santa for. And I got my holiday wish, too—what he said earlier about wanting this to be more than just one night. It feels like a miracle.

So does the way he's kissing me, soft and tender at first, growing more urgent and desperate. My hands slide down his back, feeling the muscles flexing under my palms, wanting to feel all of him.

Jack breaks the kiss, leaving me breathless and wanting more, but then he's kissing my neck, my collarbone, then between my breasts as I arch my back to try and give him the message that I'm ready for my bra to come off. Instead, he continues down, kissing my stomach, my hipbone, until he's between my legs, a finger hooked in the waistband of my panties.

Jack glances up at me, and I nod, silently giving permission.

He gives me a wicked grin before tugging down my underwear and tossing them somewhere behind him. Then he nudges my legs apart and his mouth is on me, hot and slick and perfect, making me gasp.

He hesitates for one second, and I bring my hands to his hair, holding it tight. "Don't stop."

"Not planning to," he murmurs.

I hiss out a slow breath as he dips one finger inside me, still exploring me with his mouth. When he adds a second finger, I let out a deep, guttural moan. Every nerve ending in my body is lit, like I'm a candle on the biggest menorah ever made, glowing brighter and brighter as his hands grip my hips and goosebumps travel up my legs until I come hard and fast, riding a wave of pleasure as it pulls me down and lifts me up, washing me in a warm glow.

"That was incredible," I manage to say.

Jack crawls back over me, looking more than a little smug. "You're incredible," he says, though I'm not the one responsible for the way I'm feeling right now.

"Do you have a condom?" I raise my eyebrows.

Jack pauses, scrunching up his forehead. "Here? Now?" He glances down at himself. "Somehow tucked into my underwear that you didn't notice when you had your hand and mouth on me a few minutes ago?"

I laugh, shaking my head. "My roommate has some," I say, and climb off the bed, still a little lightheaded.

I hesitate at the door, turning to see Jack on his back in my bed, his hair a wild mess, wearing nothing but those reindeer boxer briefs I am desperate to get off him as soon as possible. I point at him, grinning. "Don't move."

I duck into Julie's room and open her dresser drawer. I start to tear off one foil package but opt to grab the whole strip—just in case.

When I return, Jack is just where I left him, and a grin lights up his face when I hold up the entire strip of condoms.

"It's a Hannukah miracle," he says.

I launch myself onto the bed next to him, laughing when he grabs me around the waist and pulls me on top of him so I'm straddling him.

He reaches for the clasp of my bra, that mischievous gleam in his eyes again. "You look absolutely stunning in this, but it needs to come off."

I agree completely, and together, we yank off my bra, tossing it on the floor. Immediately, his hands are on my breasts and he's groaning as his eyes flutter shut. "I was right," he says in a strained voice. "This is even better."

I lean down as he lifts his head, taking my nipple in his mouth, giving it a soft bite before switching to the other side, making me gasp.

"What about these," I say, scooching down and tugging at his boxer briefs. "Super cute, but…"

"Take 'em off."

I slide off the bed as he lifts his hips, helping me strip off the boxers and throw them aside. Then he shifts so he's sitting on the edge of the bed and I'm facing him, both of us completely bare. And it hits me all over again: *damn,* is he gorgeous. Best of all, he's staring at me like he's ready to devour me again.

The streetlamps outside my window are the only source of light, giving my room an almost ethereal glow. I shiver, thinking about the magic and the miracle of this season, and how everything that went wrong—my roommates leaving me alone, the storm, Jack missing his flight, the power going out—led to this beautiful moment.

There will be enough. Enough light and enough love. And enough time. Even though Jack is leaving tomorrow morning, he's coming back. And he doesn't want this to be a one-time thing, either.

Then I rip open a foil package and roll the condom down his length, making him sigh with pleasure. I slide onto his lap and reach down, positioning him where I need him to be. Slowly, I sink down as he stretches and fills me.

"Perfect," he groans, pressing his forehead against mine, his muscles tensing as he holds me in place. "Nessa, you're perfect. Exactly what I want."

And I believe him—that for the first time in so long, I feel like I'm someone's first choice. Like I'm not too much. I'm just exactly enough.

Then he captures my mouth in a deep, searching kiss. My body hums with pleasure, and I shift my hips in circles, feeling the friction as we continue to kiss. Jack slides his hand down to cup my ass, lifting me up, then pressing into me as deep as he can go. I meet him, thrust for thrust, my back arching and my mind going hazy until—

Suddenly, he's standing with me in his arms, turning us around and setting me down again on my back, flat on the mattress, looking up at him. Jack's bracing himself above me, a naughty smile on his face.

"How are we doing?" he asks, parting my legs and sliding into me again.

I let out a quiet moan, my hands gripping the sheets. "So—so nice," I manage.

"Well, we can do better than *nice*." He bends my knee up against him before thrusting into me again, harder.

This time, I moan out loud, and he gives a grunt of satisfaction. I'm mesmerized by the sight of him, watching the muscles in his chest and shoulders tense, his brow furrow in concentration, like he's trying to hold himself back, to make sure I come first—again. And it's that knowledge, combined with the way he's hitting just the right spot, that brings me to the edge for the second time tonight.

He leans down to kiss me, and my body clenches tight around

him, urging him deeper, harder, faster. I feel him start to shudder. He's there. I'm there. The two of us, tumbling together off a cliff into a freefall that is terrifying and exciting all at once. Because somehow, deep down, I know this isn't just a passing moment. It feels real. Lasting. Like we've started something that will stay with us both, long after tonight.

CHAPTER 17

DECEMBER 26, 6:39 am
JACK

*M*y eyes flutter open in the darkness, and it takes a few moments for reality to settle in. I'm in Nessa's bed, her body curled against mine, her breathing deep and even. I close my eyes again, letting last night replay in my mind—the taste of her, the warmth of her, and the simple, perfect joy of falling asleep with her.

But now it's morning, and a rock of dread settles in my chest.

I reach for my phone, the screen lighting up with the text from my dad: details for my flight. It leaves in less than four hours. I should feel excited—eager to get up, shower, pack, and head home to see my family. That's the plan I've had for months.

Instead, I feel...torn.

I glance at Nessa, still sleeping peacefully, and imagine what we could do if I stayed. Three whole days together before real life comes crashing down again—slow mornings, long conversations, maybe a movie or dinner out. But more than anything, just being here. Talking. Laughing. Getting to know each other better.

But my parents are expecting me, and I hate the thought of disappointing them—even though, at this point, I'll be there for barely more than forty-eight hours before I have to turn around and leave again. My sister and her kids will have gone home to Grand Junction. I've already missed all the holiday traditions.

And when I return, it'll be right back to the grind of residency with hardly a chance to catch my breath. My mom's words from our call yesterday come into my mind: *Do what's best for you, okay?*

The problem is, I don't know what that is—I've spent these past few months ignoring my wants and needs, throwing everything I've got into taking care of my patients to the best of my ability.

Nessa stirs beside me, her hand brushing my shoulder. "Hey," she whispers, her voice husky with sleep. "You awake?"

I roll toward her, smiling as her face comes into focus. "Good morning, beautiful."

She burrows into my chest, wrapping her arms around me. "When do you have to go?"

I exhale slowly. "Flight leaves just after ten."

"Oh."

The disappointment in her tone echoes my own.

"I'll be back on the twenty-eighth," I say, trying to ignore the fact that I'll get home around nine p.m. and have to be up at five the next morning. "Can I see you that night?"

"You better," she says, glancing up at me with a soft smile.

"It's a date, then." I press a kiss to the top of her head. "Our fifth, I think?"

She chuckles and nestles against me again. "What are you doing on New Year's Eve? My roommates and I are throwing a party. I'd love for you to come. Meet everyone."

My throat tightens. "I can't," I say, hating the words even as they leave my mouth. "That's when I start night shift. Seven to seven, for a month."

She pulls away, propping herself on one elbow and brushing her hair out of her face. "A whole month? I don't even get home from work until six-thirty or seven, usually. Do you have weekends off, at least?"

I shake my head. "Just Wednesdays."

Her expression falls, and it hits me—what she said about never being anyone's favorite. She almost seems to be bracing herself, expecting to be let down. Her roommates both left, her parents are on vacation together, and Nessa hasn't said a word of complaint, but deep down, I'm sure she feels abandoned. Like everyone else has somewhere better to be. I hate that I'm the one making her feel that way again.

"This is why I didn't try to meet you before," I tell her. "I wanted to—but I knew it'd be hard. My life...it doesn't leave much room for anything else."

"I get it," she says softly. "It's okay."

"I'm sorry, Nessa."

My words can't begin to capture how sorry I truly am. I've only just started getting to know her and already real life is barging in. I'm leaving, and when I get back, we'll hardly see each other. What if, after spending this perfect night together, I never really get a chance with her? It feels like such a terrible waste. This spark between us, blown out before it even has an opportunity to grow.

But it would be crazy to change my plans for a girl I just met. Right? Kind of like how it was crazy to knock on her door in the first place.

She gives me a small, tight smile that doesn't reach her eyes. "It's really okay. You should get ready for your flight."

I pull her close again, pressing a kiss to her lips, then her jaw, her neck, nipping at her soft skin with my teeth and making her laugh.

"I think I can spare fifteen minutes," I say. "If you're up for that?"

"I am *so* up for that."

IN MY APARTMENT, I move on autopilot—shower, get dressed, check my bag. I glance out the window near my bed. The sky is a pale gray, the city beginning to wake.

My mind drifts back to how I felt when I first arrived here. The anxiety, the uncertainty, questioning why I'd even applied to a residency so far away from home. And every day since, my doubt has deepened.

Meeting Nessa is the first time I've felt like maybe there's a reason I'm here.

Shaking my head, I sit on the edge of my bed and pull on my shoes. I've seen too much tragedy and suffering in residency to believe that everything happens for a reason.

But then I think back to my conversation with Nessa as we lit the candles last night. Finding light in the darkness. Hope, even in the worst of times. Trusting that what we have—and who we are—will be enough.

I've never been one to dig too deep into the meaning of Christmas. Growing up, my family read the stories—about shepherds seeing angels, wise men following a star—but they always just felt like words. Now, I think I'm finally getting it. The heart of the holidays isn't in flawless plans or finding the perfect gifts. It's in the unexpected—the surprises you never saw coming, the unplanned moments that shift your perspective and change the way you see the world.

Like meeting someone who makes one night celebrating two holidays feel like the start of something bigger.

Maybe that's the real message: that the best things come when you let go of expectations and stay open to whatever life brings your way. That even when the path feels uncertain, it might lead you exactly where you need to be.

And I know where I need to be.

CHAPTER 18

December 26, 8:37 am
NESSA

*I*n my head, I know we need darkness to appreciate light. The contrast is essential. One can't exist without the other. Like if I hadn't known the deep loneliness of being left behind by my roommates, then Jack's arrival—shivering with his comforter wrapped around him—wouldn't have felt quite so sweet.

Unfortunately, the opposite is also true. And going from the warm after-glow of having Jack in my bed, the way he lit me up from the inside out, making me feel worthy and beautiful and chosen to lying here alone is just torture.

Tears fill my eyes. Even as they spill down my cheeks, I know this is ridiculous. Jack had to go—the holidays are for spending time with your family, the people you love most in the world. And he already pushed his plans back for one night.

He doesn't know that I know. To be fair, I had no clue when he first told me the airport was still closed, that he wouldn't be leaving until this morning. But when I was on my phone looking for a latke recipe, I saw a news alert that O'Hare had been reopened hours earlier with flights going in and out.

Which means Jack could have gone home and salvaged the rest of his holiday, but instead, he stayed in this frozen tundra with me so we could get to know each other. So I wouldn't be alone on Hanukkah.

I got a whole extra night, and I know that should be enough. It would be selfish to want more—Jack has a whole family who misses him. Plus, he's coming back.

The thought doesn't comfort me—the tears keep coming, and hiccuping sobs roll through me. My bed just feels so empty without him, and I know the days ahead are going to feel endlessly long. Not to mention, being lonely hurts even more now that I know how good it felt to have Jack here with me.

Two days will go by in a flash, I try to convince myself. And he's already promised we'll go on a real date. We'll get dressed up and go out to dinner, and then after, we'll come back here and stay up all night, exploring each other's bodies, learning all the ways we can feel even more connected. Hell, maybe we'll skip the dinner out and eat one of his frozen dinners in bed.

The thought of Jack eating Salisbury steak that isn't even steak makes me cry even harder because I know how busy he's going to be. He all but said he won't have any time for me, and what kind of relationship is that? I almost wish I didn't know how good we could be together if we'll just fizzle out like a match once real life kicks in.

Except, I wouldn't trade the last two days for anything. Even if it means living with the ache of knowing these magical moments will only exist in our memories. It was worth the risk. The way Jack made me feel was worth risking everything—even the sadness of having to say goodbye.

I'm crying so hard it takes me a second to register the sound of someone knocking at my door.

I pull the comforter over my head—the only person I want to

see is at the airport, probably going through security at this very moment. Everyone else I even remotely care about is off celebrating and spending time with the ones they love most.

The knocking is getting louder and more persistent, and I'm suddenly furious at whoever is out there, making it impossible for me to fall apart in peace. I toss back the comforter and throw on a T-shirt before storming into the living room.

"Who is it?" I shout, not bothering to hide my annoyance.

"It's…uh…the snowman destroyer."

Confused, I fling the front door open.

It's Jack.

Jack with his messy dark hair and electric blue eyes, his hands outstretched and a big smile on his face.

But when he sees my face—probably red and blotchy from all the crying—his smile vanishes. "Nessa…"

"What are you doing here?" I ask, my voice catching. "You're going to miss your flight."

He brings his hands up to cup my face, his gaze steady and warm and gentle. "I was going to miss you more."

His thumbs brush away the remnants of my tears, and if he were anyone else, I'd be embarrassed by the evidence of my emotional breakdown. But it's Jack.

Jack, who made me feel safe enough to make the first move.

Jack, who turned a frozen dinner into a beautiful memory.

Jack, who made me feel, for the first time, like I'm worth choosing. Like I'm not too much—like I'm just right.

A small sob escapes me as I wrap my arms around him. He holds me close, whispering in my ear that this is exactly where he wants to be, telling me about all the things he hopes we'll do together. That he didn't want to miss this chance to spend more time with me.

"What about your family?" I ask, blinking up at him through my tears. "The holiday?"

Jack shrugs. "I'll visit them for Arbor Day."

Before I can ask him who celebrates Arbor Day, his lips are on mine. This kiss isn't like our last one. It isn't a goodbye, it's a promise. It's hello again. It says I choose you, and it says this is just the beginning.

EPILOGUE

December 24, 2027, 4:14 pm
NESSA

"*T*ime to wake up, beautiful."

I smile and snuggle deeper under the blanket, not ready to end this glorious nap yet. We're in Colorado at Jack's family cabin up in the mountains—we took the first flight out of Chicago at the crack of dawn this morning, just in case another massive snowstorm tried to ruin our plans.

It's not my first time spending the holidays with Jack's family, but it's the first time in three years that our holidays are overlapping again—this time, with Christmas Eve on the first night of Hanukkah. Only the fifth time in the last one hundred years. His parents invited my parents to join us this year, and the blended families seem to be working out as well as our blended holidays.

"I think the eggnog is ready, and so are the latkes," Jack says, brushing his lips against mine.

"Mmm." I slip my arms around his neck and bring his mouth back to mine. My lips part, and when our tongues meet, I feel the same spark I felt after our first kiss.

It's crazy, thinking back on everything that's happened in the past three years. Our first few months together were a little tricky—Jack was so busy at the hospital, still finding his footing as a resident. But we made it work, even if it meant sneaking in a quick shower together after his overnight shifts and before I had to rush off to work. On the plus side, it forced us to slow things down, to build a solid foundation from the beginning.

A year after we started dating, both my roommates moved out—Amanda with her fiancé and Julie, into a high-rise with an in-unit washer/dryer and a pool—so Jack moved in. That made it even easier for us to support each other—I helped him through the rest of his residency, and he supported me through an unexpected job layoff. Jack graduated last summer (he was voted Resident of the Year, no surprise to me), and I found a position at a new agency I love. And a few months ago, Jack landed his first "real job" as an attending at a nearby hospital and we moved into a much nicer apartment in Lincoln Park.

And to think, none of it would've happened without that snowstorm.

"I'm so glad the power went out and you got stranded in Chicago that Christmas," I say, snuggling against him.

He chuckles, kissing my forehead. "Me, too. Though I'm sorry I even considered leaving you—I'll never forget how awful I felt when I came back and saw that you'd been crying."

"I'm actually glad you left."

Jack huffs, surprised. "What?"

I roll over, propping myself up on my elbow so I can look at him. "Sometimes staying is the path of least resistance; it's a passive choice. But leaving and coming back? That was an active choice."

Jack rests his hand on my hip, drawing slow circles with his thumb as he pulls me closer. "I will always choose you. Because I love you the most."

"No way," I tease, grinning. This is my favorite argument of ours. "I love *you* the most."

His eyes sparkle, and without warning, he rolls on top of me, pinning me against the mattress. I laugh, squirming beneath him.

"Sorry, no," he says, dead serious. "I love you more than anyone has ever loved any other person in the entire history of the universe and that's an actual fact—don't argue with me; I have citations."

My heart swells as I look up at him. I can see all the love in his eyes, all the work we've put into building what we have together —and everything I'm looking forward to in the future.

"Fine," I whisper, surrendering. "You win."

Then he captures my mouth in a deep kiss and quickly makes me forget that we're supposed to be joining our families soon.

"JACKY!" His mom's voice breaks through our perfect little bubble, and I groan. "THE LAT-KEYS ARE GETTING COLD!"

Jack smiles, giving me another quick kiss before folding the comforter back. "We can't have cold latkes. And by the way—it looks like my mom is a sour cream goy."

"No," I gasp, shaking my head in mock disappointment. "And your dad?"

"Applesauce." He grabs my hand and leads me down the hall.

Downstairs, the living room is the best kind of chaos. My heart swells as I take it all in, the fire roaring in the fireplace, and the sound of laughter and Christmas music filling the air. My dad is on the couch, next to Jack's sister Nic, her husband Eddie, and her two kids—10-year-old Gabrielle and six-year-old Sammy. The kids' heads are bent in concentration as they take turns trying to spin the dreidel.

"Auntie Nessa!" Gabrielle shouts. "I got a Gimmel!"

Jack catches my eye and grins—neither of us can look at a dreidel without remembering what our first game led to— and I swallow a laugh. "Good job, bud!"

"Come play!"

"Later," Jack's mom says, popping her head out of the kitchen. "Latkes are ready, and then we have to light the candles."

"Birthday candles?" Sammy says.

Gabrielle shakes her head at him. "No, Hanukkah candles, dummy."

Sammy's lower lip starts to quiver, but Unca-Jack swoops him up and carries him to the kitchen, saving the day. "Let's see what kind of goy you are..."

The latkes are delicious—our moms cooked them together using real Idaho potatoes. Not a frozen spud in sight.

Once the latke appetizers have been devoured and washed down with eggnog, it's time to light the candles. I offered to bring my menorah with us, but Jack's mom wanted to have one to keep here for future holidays.

I liked the idea of that, spending future holidays here with Jack and his family, the lights on their Christmas tree and the candles on the menorah shining bright in their window. Before the little kids go to bed, we'll light Jack's mom's Advent wreath and set out cookies for Santa. And then maybe Jack and I will play a little strip dreidel on our own.

But first, Hanukkah. With Jack's family and my family gathered around me, I light the shamash. My parents and I say the blessing, and Jack's family repeats each phrase after us. Everyone but Sammy, who is singing the Happy Birthday song.

We invite Jack's mom to light the candles, and she looks deeply honored as she takes the shamash from my hand and uses it to light the first night's candle.

"Now, let's eat!" Eddie says, corralling the kids into the dining room. The others follow, leaving Jack and I alone.

"Happy Hanukkah," he says, giving me a kiss and handing me a wrapped box the size of an orange.

"What's this?" We agreed to open presents with everyone tomorrow on Christmas morning and saved a few for the last nights of Hanukkah back home.

"It's a Hanukkah present." There's a nervous glint in his eyes. "Open it."

"Jack…"

"Let's sit."

I follow him toward the couch, my stomach flipping with apprehension and anticipation. "What did you do?" I ask as I untie the elaborate ribbons—blue and white and red and green. I open the top of the box and laugh—it's filled with Hershey's kisses.

"Almost exactly what I wanted," I say, echoing his words from long ago.

Jack nods at the box. "There's more."

Below the first layer of chocolates, I find a bright yellow and green compression sock.

"Look inside," he says, and I slip my hand inside the sock, all the way down to the toes, where my fingers touch something cool and smooth.

A ring.

My breath catches as I pull it out, and I look up to see Jack, down on bended knee and gazing up at me, his blue eyes shining.

"Some might say it took an act of nature to bring us together," he says, his voice low and steady. "But if you ask me, it was a miracle. Nessa, when we met, I was at the lowest point in my life, wondering if I was on the wrong path—but meeting you changed all that."

Tears fill my eyes as I slip off the couch and kneel across from him.

"You showed me that what I have to offer is enough," he continues. "You taught me that even in the toughest moments, there's always hope." He clears his throat, his own eyes shimmering. "You're my light in the darkness. My miracle. And I don't want to face a day without you by my side. Will you choose me, for the rest of our lives?"

"Always and forever," I say, and he slips the ring on my finger before pulling me into a kiss.

"She said yes!" Nic shouts, and we're suddenly surrounded by our family, laughter and cheers filling the room. I hold out my hand, letting everyone see the ring. The diamond shines as brightly as the menorah, casting rainbows across the room.

I look at Jack, at our families celebrating around us, and I feel like I'm getting a glimpse of our future. Our families getting closer, our traditions intertwining. Our own family growing as we add a baby or two of our own; the noise and the chaos and love growing every year. And I realize that this is the real miracle: not the grand gestures or perfect gifts. It's in the quiet, imperfect, everyday choices—the decision to stay, to hope, to love. It's in knowing that even when everything feels uncertain, we'll keep choosing each other. That's what keeps the light alive.

WANT **a sneak peek at the next romance from Ali Brady? Keep reading for a preview of** *Battle of the Bookstores* **(coming 6/3/25 from Berkley/Penguin Random House) and an interview with the author.**

BATTLE OF THE BOOKSTORES

Coming June 3, 2025
Keep reading for a sneak peek!

CHAPTER ONE

JOSIE

When I tell people I'm a bookseller, I'm sure they imagine me curled up in a cozy chair reading for hours, sipping coffee and discussing books, or hobnobbing with famous authors at literary events. You know, living the ultimate bookish dream, with every breath filled with that intoxicating tang of fresh ink and crisp paper.

What they don't imagine are the endless hours on my feet, my back aching from hefting twenty-pound boxes of books, or my stomach knotting from the constant stress about razor-thin profit margins and climbing overhead expenses.

Still, there's nothing else I'd rather do. I love flicking on the lights each morning and gazing at the shelves and stacks, all neat lines and sharp corners. I love unpacking shipments of glossy new hardcovers and recommending my favorites to customers.

But the best part—the absolute, hands-down, best part of running a bookstore—is getting to read books before they come out.

Several months before publication, publishers send galleys to booksellers, advanced reading copies that arrive in brown paper packages, covers adorned with glowing blurbs, in the hopes that we'll read and recommend (and hopefully stock multiple copies of) this new title.

A while back, a publicist at one of my favorite imprints emailed to ask if I'd consider reading an upcoming release and providing a quote, if I liked it. And did I? Well, I stayed up until three o'clock in the morning reading, and my tears left damp spots on the final pages. I spent days writing and rewriting the perfect paragraph to encapsulate the essence of this epic, heart-wrenching story.

Last week, I got an email from said publicist telling me that advance copies were being sent out, and oh, by the way, they'd used my quote on the back cover (cue internal squeeing!). This morning, that package arrived. My hands shake as I rip open the brown paper, my eyes scanning until—

"A stunning meditation on grief and betrayal. . . . Worth reading and cherishing for years to come."
—Josie Klein, bookseller
Tabula Inscripta, Somerville, MA

My breath rushes out. They only used a fraction of the paragraph I sent.

But: It's my quote. My name. I've spent the past five years becoming the best bookseller I can be, determined to prove that a college dropout can make something of her life. I may be a bookish little introvert, but I've got ideas and opinions to share. Someday, I hope readers throughout the city—maybe even the country—will turn to me for book recommendations.

Someday, my voice will matter.

Desperate to share my excitement, I grab my phone and pull up BookFriends, a website with discussion forums for book-sellers across the country.

BookshopGirl: Guess who got an ARC with her first blurb printed on it?!

I post it in the Celebration subforum, where any user can read it, but I'm hoping to reach one specific person. Biting my lip in anticipation, I wait—and when I see the username I'm looking for, my heart soars.

RJ.Reads: What?? Congratulations! That's amazing! Just wish you could tell us the title so I could see it.

I wish I could, too, but the forums are strictly anonymous. That way, booksellers can share honest opinions about publishers and authors without fear of negative blowback.

Grinning, I switch over to our DM thread.

> BookshopGirl: There's only one other bookseller quoted on the back of this ARC and guess who it is?

RJ.Reads: PAW?

> BookshopGirl: You got it!

RJ knows all about my adoration of Penelope Adler-Wolf, owner of Wolf Books in Providence, Rhode Island. PAW is a bookseller of impeccable taste and vast influence. If she endorses a book, it's gonna be Big. My goal in life is to be just like her.

My phone lights up again with a reminder: MEETING WITH XANDER.

I sigh. Xander Laing has spent the past few years buying up the entire block, including the coffee shop next door, though he doesn't care about books or coffee—just his bottom line. When he bought Tabula Inscripta, Xander questioned if "a girl with nothing but a high school diploma" could handle being the manager. I convinced him to give me a shot and since I pull a profit each month, he keeps me around. Still, I always feel like I'm on thin ice.

I send a message to RJ, wishing I could chat longer.

BookshopGirl: Gotta go—have a great morning!

RJ.Reads: You too. And congrats again. I'm so happy for you.

After that, I lock the door behind me and step into a crisp, sunlit morning. My bookstore is right in the heart of Davis Square, my favorite neighborhood in the Boston area—tree-lined streets, brick-paved sidewalks, charming shops, and eclectic restaurants. It's late May and the day is already warm, the air filled with the gentle hum of traffic and the occasional ting of a bicycle bell.

I step into Beans, where I breathe in the life-giving aroma of coffee. Xander's not here yet, thankfully.

"Josie!" Eddie Callahan, the manager, calls. His classic Southie accent, tattoos, and gruff exterior hide the fact that he's a total softie. "Good mornin', sweetheart. The usual?"

"Yes, please," I say, smiling as I walk up to the counter. "How's the morning rush going?"

"Nearly over, thank god." Eddie motions over his shoulder at a blonde barista, who's struggling with the complicated espresso machine. "You know how it is—you hire someone, hoping to get some help, and it ends up taking ten times as much energy to train 'em." He shakes his head. "I shouldn't complain when you're staffing that place alone seven days a week."

"My sister helps when she can," I say.

Eddie gives me a worried-uncle look. "You're gonna burn yourself out, kid. Let's get you an extra shot of espresso and a cheese croissant. On the house." He winks.

He fusses over me like a mother hen, and I love him for it—my own mom never did, and his concern unexpectedly makes my throat tighten.

"You're the best," I say.

"That's a fact." Another wink. "I'll have Mabel bring your order. Good luck with the boss man today."

I thank him and turn. Xander's arrived; he's seated at a table next to a man whose back is to me.

"Good morning," I say as I pull up a chair.

Xander—short and balding and with a perpetual irritated frown—gives me a curt nod, then motions between me and the other guy. "I assume you two know each other?"

"No," I say, as the guy turns and says, "Yes."

I blink, confused. He does seem familiar, but I can't place him. He's around my age, with messy brown hair and tortoiseshell glasses. He's wearing a brown cardigan and a pink lanyard stuck all over with colorful pins. I assume the lanyard holds a name tag, but it's flipped around, so that's no help.

Xander is introducing us, but I only snap to attention as he says, "—and this is Josie Klein, who manages Tabula Inscripta."

"I'm so sorry," I say, embarrassed. "I don't remember meeting you before."

This isn't unusual for me—sometimes I'm so deep into a book that even when I'm not reading, my mind is stuck on the story and I can have a whole conversation and hardly remember it.

The guy blinks at me from behind his glasses, a confused smile tugging at his lips. "I manage . . . Happy Endings?"

He points to his right, the opposite side of the coffee shop from my store.

It all clicks, and my stomach drops. He's the tall guy who runs the romance bookstore on the other side of Beans. Eddie once told me he made some comment about how there's "not enough caffeine in the entire coffee shop to keep people awake while reading the books sold at the Tab." Eddie thought it was funny, but it hit a nerve. I grew up being teased about my adoration for books that put everyone else to sleep. And sure, literary fiction isn't everyone's cup of tea, but coming from a fellow bookseller? That stung.

"Oh, right," I say. "The massage place around the corner?"

It's supposed to be a joke, and maybe a little payback, but the man's smile drops abruptly.

"It's a bookstore," he says.

Apparently, this guy can dish it out, but he sure can't take it. Or maybe I'm "not that funny," as I've been told plenty of times. Guess that's what happens when you spend your formative years inhaling books rather than learning how to, you know, people.

"I—I know," I say awkwardly. "You just sell romance."

His jaw tightens, and I realize my error—I didn't mean just romance like I'm disparaging the genre, I meant romance is the only genre he sells.

This is going all wrong—I'm operating at peak social awkwardness today; usually I enjoy making connections with other people in the industry.

"Let's start over," I say, sticking my hand out. What did Xander say his name was? Brian? "It's nice to officially meet you, Brian. I'm Josie."

He gives me a tentative shake. His hand is huge, engulfing mine. "I know who you are, and it's—"

"Great, we all know each other," Xander says, interrupting. "But I've called you both here for a reason."

I turn to face him, pull out my notebook, and write the date in the top right corner. I consider writing BRIAN, too, so I can commit the name to memory, but I'm worried he'll see it.

"Here you go!" a cheery voice says, and I look up to see the new barista, Mabel. She sets a drink in front of me. "An iced white-chocolate-chunk macchiato with two extra pumps of vanilla, miss."

"Oh, this isn't mine," I say, handing it back to her. "I had an Americano?"

Mabel gasps. "I'm sorry! Eddie said to bring it to this table, I figured since you're the only woman here—"

"It's mine," Brian mumbles.

Xander chuckles. "Should've been obvious—he's the one who works at the girly bookstore."

Mabel scurries off as Brian's ears turn pink. My stomach clenches. I know how it feels to be on the receiving end of Xander's digs.

"Xander," I say, "that's not—"

"And your coffee order is like your books, right, Josie?" Xander continues, grinning. "Boring and bitter. What'd you call her store, Lawson? A bleak wasteland of existential dread?"

He laughs and nudges Brian, who huffs out a half laugh before stopping himself. But he doesn't correct Xander.

I press my lips together, seething. I won't make the mistake of feeling bad for him again.

Xander's phone buzzes on the table and he answers it, holding up a finger to indicate that we should wait. Then he stands and walks a few steps away, barking into his phone about a construction project.

Mabel reappears with my drink. "Here you go—Americano, no milk, no sugar."

"Thanks," I say.

Brian's lips twitch, like he's trying not to smirk. Probably thinking his good pal Xander really nailed me: Boring and bitter.

I know I should ignore him, but this guy is getting to me. So many people see a buttoned-up bookseller and assume I'm timid. But when it comes to defending my store—and the stories within it—I don't hold back.

I face him. "Excuse me?"

"I didn't say anything."

"Well, you sure seem to have an opinion about my coffee choice." And my books. "Please, do share."

Brian blinks and licks his lips. "Just wondering . . . does anyone actually enjoy that kind of drink? Or do they order it because"—his eyes flick toward my store—"they think it impresses other people?"

My jaw tightens. I've always believed that book people are the best people, but there's an exception to every rule.

"Maybe I've learned to appreciate complex, nuanced flavors," I say, and take a sip of my Americano. It burns my tongue, and I wince.

His eyebrows lift.

"It's hot," I say, too defensively.

"Okay." He takes a long, long sip of his drink and I suppress a sigh, telling myself not to let him get under my skin.

When Brian sets his cup down, there's a dot of whipped cream on his upper lip. My eyes zero in as his tongue slips out and licks the cream away. Something prickles across my skin, like static electricity.

I shake myself and look away.

"What?" he says.

"Nothing. Just seems like you're really enjoying your drink."

"I am."

"Great. It's important to know what you like, Brian—"

"You have no idea what I like," he says, eyes flashing. "You don't even know my—"

"Can we keep moving?" Xander says, returning to his seat. As if we're the ones who interrupted the meeting.

"Absolutely," I say, picking up my pen again and facing him. The sooner this ends, the sooner I can go back to avoiding Brian. "You had something to talk with us about?"

"Yes," Xander says. "I'm combining your stores and Beans."

Brian chokes on his drink.

I stare at Xander. "Combine . . . our stores?"

Xander nods. "It's been my plan all along, and the pieces are finally falling into place. This neighborhood doesn't need two bookstores so close together. It's bad for business, built-in competition."

I'm about to tell him that my clientele is entirely different from that of a romance bookstore, but Xander's still talking.

"And you know what people like to do when they shop for books? Drink coffee. Eddie says customers are always coming here and reading. So I figured, hey, let's combine it all. One big bookstore with a coffee shop in the middle. People can get Harry Potters and parenting books and spy thrillers and sit right down and read them. You know?"

I'm speechless. Appalled. A little nauseated.

Tabula Inscripta has always been a small, boutique bookstore focusing on literary fiction and select non-fiction. I spend hours each season curating my selection, just as the prior owner, Jerome, taught me. I imagine his bushy gray eyebrows rising in horror at all these changes.

"But our bookstores are totally different," Brian says.

"Yes, completely different customer bases," I say, nodding. "We're not in competition."

"Well, you'll figure it out," Xander says. "I mean, one of you will."

I blanch. "What?"

"No reason for me to pay two managers for one store."

"So—one of us is out of a job?" Brian sounds horrified.

"Who?" I ask, instantly sick. Xander is a man's man. I know he's going to choose Brian—the two of them already seem chummy.

"I'm not deciding right now," Xander says. "Here's the plan."

He launches into a detailed explanation, and I do my best to take notes, even though my head is spinning. Construction will start in a couple of weeks, and the stores will stay open during the process. Xander anticipates the process taking three months, and the manager who earns the most profit during that period will be the manager of the new store. The other will be looking for a new job.

"So you'll hire either Brian or me, based solely on financials?" I hate the idea of being judged by profit—if Xander knew anything about bookselling, he'd know that owning an indie bookstore will never make him rich—but at least it's an objective measure.

Brian frowns. "It's actually—"

"Exactly," Xander interrupts. "I anticipate making my decision by Labor Day."

I sneak a glance at Brian. I can't get a bead on him. The cardigan, lanyard, and tortoiseshell glasses are giving "small-town librarian," which isn't a terrible vibe for a bookseller. The messy hair, I'll admit, bothers me; he can't take the time to comb his hair before work? But maybe that's a good thing—maybe he's a mess in other aspects of his life, including his managerial skills.

Brian's eyes flick over to meet mine. My skin prickles again. Behind his glasses, his eyes are warm golden brown, like dark honey, and my stomach coils tight with the strangest sensation. For one split second, I get a flash of us sitting at this table, each with a coffee and a book, reading together.

Ha. No way—he'd probably make snarky comments about my book being better than Ambien.

Plus, he's my competition.

Brian shifts his weight, which makes his lanyard slip forward, revealing some of the colorful pins. They say things like MORALLY GRAY >>>, BOOK WHORE, IN MY SMUT ERA, SPREAD THOSE PAGES.

And one that I cannot for the life of me understand: STFU-ATTDLAGG.

Focus, I tell myself. This man has disparaged my books, my store, and my personality. Now he could end up with my job? Everything I've worked for in the past five years, the reputation I've built, the clientele I've cultivated—all my goals for the future are riding on this. I've pulled myself out of the humiliating hole of my past to create a career I'm proud of.

I can't let this guy take that away.

At least my chances of winning are decent. I mean, how many books could a romance bookstore sell, anyway?

CHAPTER TWO

RYAN

She's called me Brian three times.

Make that four.

I always figured Josie—see, I know her name—didn't like me. She gives me the cold shoulder every time I see her at Beans. Acts like she doesn't know who I am.

Maybe it's not an act?

Which would be crazy. She's worked at the Tab almost as long as I've been running Happy Endings. I know she orders an Americano with three shots of espresso in the morning and herbal tea in the afternoon. And a cookie if she's having a bad day.

Although, TBH, it always looks like she's having a bad day.

Maybe her bun is too tight. I get the sense Josie never lets her hair down—literally or figuratively. I don't think I've ever seen her without a thick book in her hands. It's like she carts them around to make sure everyone knows she's Smart with a capital S.

It's obvious she is. She's also really pretty, in an unapproachable, ice-queen way. Dark hair and sharp green eyes, wearing heels so high they could be used as shivs.

Which is why I've never had the balls to talk to her.

And I probably won't have the chance to ever again after Xander's comment. I did not describe her bookstore as "a bleak wasteland of existential dread." I said her bookstore is bleak—an objective fact—and her books fill me with existential dread. Also true.

Okay, so maybe that's not any better. I still wish I'd corrected him.

"I'm glad you two are being good sports about this," Xander says.

Josie has her arms crossed over her chest, her jaw clenched tight. I can't tell if she's scowling or trying to hold back tears.

"Doesn't seem like we have a choice," I say.

Xander laughs as if I've made a joke. This whole meeting feels like a joke, and we're the punch line. I can picture him with his smug grin, lying naked in a California King bed, counting his money and thinking of ways to make his monkeys dance.

I don't want to dance for him or anyone else, and I don't want to compete against Josie for our jobs. I wish there was a way we could both win and no one would lose their store.

But the world isn't all happy endings, dickwad.

I shake my head, trying to clear my older brothers' words from my mind. They'd probably be happy to see me lose and get a more "masculine" job, one that won't make them question my sexuality or the fact that I'm single.

The store must be crawling with hotties.

If I were you, I'd be banging a different customer every day.

Sometimes it blows my mind that we grew up in the same house with the same parents and ended up with such different ideas about love and sex.

"All right then." Xander scoots his chair back so abruptly it screeches against the floor. Josie cringes, revealing a dimple I've never noticed. She really is pretty; even when she's upset. "May the best bookseller win."

And with that, he's off.

I turn back to Josie, hoping for a moment of shared commiseration, but she's eyeing me like I'm the enemy.

I should say something to break the tension, but I don't have a clever bone in my giant, awkward body. Especially around a woman who's as intimidating as she is striking. *The Hating Game* comes to mind, and I wonder what Josh Templeman might say to Lucy Hutton in this situation. But I'm no Josh, and I don't have Sally Thorne drafting my dialogue.

My silence seems to annoy Josie even more. She stands in a huff and hurries back to her store, leaving me with a table full of dirty dishes and a familiar, soul-deep discomfort.

Growing up as the youngest of four boys, everything was a competition. Who could eat the most the fastest, who could hit the hardest, who could pee the farthest from the toilet bowl. Who was the oldest. (That one didn't make any sense.)

I came in last for every single one.

Not that I ever really tried to win. I've always gotten more pleasure from doing an activity than coming in first. What was there to even win? Bragging rights?

Now, though, the stakes couldn't be higher.

I glance at the wall dividing my store from the coffee shop, which currently displays artwork for sale by local artists. I try to picture it gone, seeing right through to Happy Endings, looking in on my employees, all blissfully unaware that everything is about to change.

Eddie and the new girl both look busy, so I bus the table and leave the dirty dishes on the counter before leaving.

The bell on the front door of Happy Endings chimes as I enter, and a wave of nostalgia hits me. Elaine, the store's original owner and my first and only boss, created this little corner of the world to be a haven for the tenderhearted: those who love love but don't always feel deserving of it. She'd be proud of how we've grown, carrying the books to back up our motto—Everyone deserves a love story.

If Happy Endings closes . . . No other bookstore in Boston carries such a diverse selection of romance. Our customers won't have anywhere to browse without judgment, to sit and read in cozy nooks, to connect with themselves and each other.

There's so much at stake, and not just for me.

"Boss!" my assistant manager shouts, even though I'm steps away from her.

"Cindy!" I say back in mock excitement. Her eyebrows furrow, and I realize my mistake. "Cinderella!"

I respect everyone's identity, and almost always get pronouns right. But for the life of me, I can't get used to calling my buxom, middle-aged, bottle-bright-red-haired assistant manager Cinderella. And it's not like she identifies as a humble, hard-working woman waiting for her prince—she just got a free name change after her divorce was final. Most people, I assume, change back to their original name, but Cinderella isn't most people.

"I got you something," she says, her eyes sparkling with mischief.

With such tenderness you'd think she was handing over the Heart of the Ocean, Cinderella places a light blue pin on my open palm.

The white letters read: NON-PRACTICING ROMANTIC.

"Get it?" Her smile lights up her face. "You'd be a practicing romantic if you ever went on a date."

"How about I'll start dating when you do?"

Cinderella blushes and shakes her head. I don't think she's been on a single date in the seven years since her divorce—right about the time she started coming into the store. Every day, she'd sit in a nook and read, crying over the happy endings. She treated her book therapy like a job, and eventually we gave her one.

I don't regret hiring Cinderella, but I do regret telling her I loved the BOSS BITCH pin she gifted me on her first day. Last I counted, I had nearly two hundred pieces of "flair." I fear the day she gives me a second lanyard.

"I saw the pin on a customer's jacket and knew it was meant for you," Cinderella says. "She didn't want to part with it, but she finally agreed to a little barter."

Persephone purrs at my feet until I pick her up. She always seems to know when I could use cheering up—unlike Hades, who keeps his distance unless I pop a can of tuna.

"A barter?" I ask, afraid to hear the details.

Cinderella shrugs. "I gave her the ARC of Ali Hazelwood's next book. I figured since we'd both read it already . . ."

"Absolutely," I say, grateful she didn't trade a book we could've sold. This penny-counting stuff is new for me—we're going to have to step it up. Tighten our bootstraps. Our belts? Whatever the metaphor, we need to do better than Josie's store and all their hardcover books with price tags as big as their authors' vocabularies. With those profit margins, she'll only have to sell half what we will.

The bell on the front door chimes, and two regular customers walk in, laughing and smiling.

"Hey, handsome." Michael is dressed as himself today, not as his alter ego Ginger, the star of our monthly Drag Queen Story Time for teens. "I'm ready for a new book boyfriend."

"I know just the guy!"

And with that, I switch gears and do what I do best: match readers with stories to help them realize they deserve the kind of love people write books about.

Seven hours later, I'm headed home, having finally finished my closing duties: including vacuuming up all the crumbs the teenagers left after camping out all afternoon in "their" reading nook.

Not that I minded. The busywork kept me from ruminating over worst-case scenarios.

Instinctively, I slow down outside Josie's store. I can see her through the window, her hair still in that severe bun, head bent over a book. I'm tempted to go inside and ask what she's reading, but I'm probably the last person she wants to talk to.

It's just . . . she looks so lonely in there.

Or maybe that's because the store is so sterile and organized it feels more like a museum than a bookstore. I shiver at the thought of her taking over Happy Endings and destroying the inclusive, beautiful selection of novels I've worked so hard to curate.

Across the street, a group of drunk college students pile out of an Uber, making enough noise to wake the dead. And attract Josie's attention.

I look away a beat too late, and as I hurry toward the Davis Square T stop, I try not to think about her sad, beautiful green eyes.

It doesn't work. I'm still thinking about them when I get home to my studio apartment in Charlestown. I pour a big glass of wine and break into the "better than sex" cookies a customer brought me today.

Desperate for a distraction, I grab my laptop and open Book-Friends, the review site for booksellers and librarians. At first, I didn't understand the strict anonymity rules, but after a popular YA author made homophobic jokes at one of my events, I realized how grateful I was for a place where I could share a warning without fear of blowback.

But my favorite thing about BookFriends is the reviews people share. It reaffirms the saying that there's a lid for every pot. What one person thinks is pure drivel is another's literary masterpiece.

There's one woman whose reviews I always look forward to. BookshopGirl reads big books like the ones Josie sells. But BSG (as I think of her) isn't a snob. Her reviews are thoughtful and inquisitive; I can tell she puts a lot of time into them.

A couple months ago, we had a lively discussion on a thread about Lily King's *Writers & Lovers*—one of the few books we've both read. The question at hand: Can a book be both literary and a romance novel? My answer was one hundred percent unequivocally yes, and after much cajoling, I got her to agree.

Someone commented and told us to "get a room"—so we did. BSG started a private message chain, and we've been chatting regularly since. In the spirit of the site, we haven't shared our names, locations, or any other personal information. Although it doesn't get more personal than sharing the books you love.

I'm relieved to see a green dot by her name; she's online. I pull up our chat and pick up where our last conversation left off: What page are you on now?

> BookshopGirl: 376.

> RJ.Reads: So you're what? Halfway done?

> BookshopGirl: More like two-thirds. I've got about 150 left.

I shake my head. A few romance novels have left me wanting more, but not three hundred pages more. Unless we're talking Lucy Score.

Good book? I ask, feeling the tension in my shoulders finally start to dissipate.

> BookshopGirl: Technically speaking, yes. The prose is beautiful and the characters are well-developed.

> RJ.Reads: And not technically speaking?

> BookshopGirl: The author is a bit pretentious—but I know that from personal experience, so I'm trying to keep an open mind about the book.

> RJ.Reads: How diplomatic of you.

BookshopGirl: I try. How about you? What page are you on?

RJ.Reads: Page zero. Finished an ARC on the way home and haven't picked my next book yet. Got a suggestion for me?

BookshopGirl: Hmmm.

As I watch the three dots appear and disappear, I smile at the prospect of reading a book of BSG's choice. Based on the books on her Favorites shelf, it might take me the whole summer to read whatever she picks, but I can always get an audio copy. Or I can do what I did during my remedial English classes in high school—google reviews and cobble together enough information to make it sound like I read the book.

Not my proudest moments.

The dots stop, then start again. I'm on the edge of my seat.

BookshopGirl: Sorry, my sister called. I've got to run, but I'll get back to you soon on a five-star book. Goodnight!

And with that, her green light turns red, and I'm left wondering what BookshopGirl's eyes look like. If they sparkle like Cinderella's, or if they're sad and lonely like Josie's.

BOOKFRIENDS

May 22, 6:47 AM

BookshopGirl: Morning! I hardly slept last night, and unfortunately I don't have a book rec for you yet, but I can share a controversial opinion inspired by recent events.

RJ.Reads: Ooh, do tell.

BookshopGirl: Books are better than people. There, I said it. Literature >>> humanity.

BookshopGirl: Now, before you think I'm a total misanthrope, I'm not saying books are better than ALL people. And it's not like I'd throw a person in front of a moving train to save a book.

RJ.Reads: But would you throw a book in front of a train to save a person?

BookshopGirl: Hmmm, depends on the person. And on the book. (Kidding. Mostly.)

BookshopGirl: I mean, I've never met a Barbara Kingsolver novel that let me down—or a person who didn't, at least a little.

RJ.Reads: I get that (though for me it's Emily Henry novels).

BookshopGirl: Books are more dependable than people. They don't stab you in the back, they don't gossip about you or insult you. Also, bonus —they won't judge you for spending the whole day in pajamas crying over the death of a character.

RJ.Reads: Or for laughing out loud in the middle of a funeral (which people definitely judge. Ask me how I know).

BookshopGirl: You read during funerals?

RJ.Reads: Just once. In my defense, it was my great-great-aunt's, and she was 102.

BookshopGirl: I'm not judging. I'm impressed.

BookshopGirl: That's another great thing about books: they're always there for you, and they'll never get sick of your company.

RJ.Reads: They'll also never complain about being ignored when life gets stressful or overwhelming.

BookshopGirl: Exactly! No matter how long it's been, books are waiting with open pages, ready to whisk you away on an adventure or comfort you after a rough day. People may come and go from your life, but books? Books are forever.

RJ.Reads: Amen to that.

CHAPTER THREE

JOSIE

Growing up, countless well-meaning adults urged me to get my "nose out of that book" and go outside to "experience real life." But from what I've seen, reality is vastly overrated.

My earliest memory is of reading Where the Wild Things Are to my sister, trying to drown out my mom's shouting match with her latest boyfriend—I couldn't even sound out all the words, but I needed to take us somewhere, anywhere, that was magical instead of messy. By second grade, when playground dynamics started to feel way too complicated, I'd spend recess lost in the pages of a chapter book. For my eleventh birthday, I invited my entire class to a Readathon party—I even reserved a room at the local library—but no one showed up. I stayed anyway, grateful for the librarians who always welcomed me. When I got to high school, I longed to go to the football games and parties everyone talked about, but I was usually home babysitting my sister. Mom wasn't exactly reliable, so someone had to be—but hey, at least I had books to keep me company.

For better or worse, my library has always grown faster than my social circle.

Managing a bookstore has forced me out of my shell, helping

me grow from a shy bookworm into someone who can confidently navigate conversations and recommendations—at least, in the safety of these shelves. Out in the world, I may be quiet and reserved, but here, I've found my voice.

Except now, Xander Laing has put all that at risk.

But it's not just my future, my livelihood—it's the customers I've served for five years. Like Beatrice Glaybold, who moved down to Florida but trusts me to send her any book I think will strike her fancy, or Michael Liu, who writes a literary column for the Boston Herald and bases his reading on my recommendations. Or James Kendall, who lost his wife last year and comes in weekly to buy a new book and chat.

If I lose this job, I lose them, too—and we all lose the store, this quiet refuge of words and stories.

When the bell on the front door chimes, I'm sitting in the back room of the shop, surrounded by boxes I haven't opened. All I can do is stare into the middle distance while panic churns in my stomach.

A voice calls, "It's me!" and a huge sigh of relief rushes out of my lungs. It's my little sister (for her, I'd throw every book I own in front of a moving train—plus myself, for good measure).

"I'm in the back!" I call.

The front door closes, followed by the familiar step-step-tap as she makes her way across the polished wood floor.

"I brought rugelach," Georgia says. She sets her cane against the desk, puts down a white to-go bag from Mamaleh's in Cambridge, and finally her backpack. She's heading to class at Tufts after this, and I feel a pinch of envy.

"Thank you, dear sister," I say, grabbing one of the pastries.

Georgia takes a bite, too, and we chew in silence. It tastes like buttery chocolate comfort. Our neighbor, Mrs. Goldstein, would bring rugelach over when our mom was having one of her "hard times"—though I doubt she had any idea how scary things could get. Georgia and I have kept up the tradition, buying it whenever one of us has a bad day.

My sister is a more relaxed, optimistic version of me, with the dark hair and green eyes we got from our dad (before he skipped out of our lives when I was five and Georgia was a baby)—but my sister's hair is loose and wild, curling from the early summer humidity. We both have the soft curves we inherited from our mom, but I'm in a tailored pencil skirt, while she's wearing a floral dress that flutters to the floor, partially obscuring the brace on her right leg. She's fearless and unguarded and fun—my opposite.

"So . . ." she says. "Didn't sleep much?"

I grimace; she's also too perceptive. Ever since she started graduate school in psychology, she's adopted a new tone that sneaks out when we're talking. Concerned; professional. Like she's trying to burrow into my brain and analyze me.

"I'm stressed," I say. "But I've been brainstorming ways to win this competition."

Georgia picks up my notebook and reads: "Number one: Cut expenses. Number two: Sell more books." She raises an eyebrow. "I hate to break it to you, Jojo, but those aren't exactly actionable strategies."

"I know," I say, sighing.

"How are you going to cut expenses? You already run this place pretty lean."

She's right. Since my part-timers left, I've been doing it all: buying, receiving, and stocking; paying the utilities; managing the website. I even clean the toilet in the back room. Georgia helps out, but she won't let me pay her. She says she "owes me for saving her life," which isn't technically true, though I appreciate the thought. What she doesn't know is that I set aside what I would have paid her in an account she can use if and when she needs it.

"And how are you going to increase your sales during the

summer?" she continues. "That's not a big season for literary fiction."

Again, she's right. This time of year, people want beach reads: light, engaging, easily digestible. I get it—sometimes people just want to unwind. What's-his-name at Happy Endings probably sells a boatload of books in the summer.

(Brian, I remind myself. Brian, who wears cardigans and weird pins and hates my bookstore. Brian, the man who has been given the power by another man to ruin my life.)

"Why couldn't this happen in the fall?" I say. My highest season for sales—aside from the holidays—is September through November, when publishers release their most anticipated titles.

"I'd be unbeatable."

"Maybe you should lean into that," Georgia says. "Target people who prefer reading books that require you to have a dictionary on hand?"

She's teasing me, but it's not a bad idea. "Maybe I could host a literary salon where people can discuss books they're reading?"

A banging sound distracts us: someone knocking on the glass door of the store. When I step out of the back room, a man is peering in the window. He waves, so I head to the door and open it a crack, trying not to let the AC escape (Strategy 1: Cut Expenses).

"Hi there, we're not open yet—"

"I need to return a book." He's the picture of impatience—crisp suit, shiny shoes, probably on his way to a Very Important Meeting—and I decide it's easier to do the return than tell him to come back later. He's not a regular customer, but if he has a good experience, maybe he'll become one (Strategy 2: Sell More Books).

I give him my most welcoming smile. "Of course. Come on in."

He follows me to the register and plunks the book down. It's the latest Oprah's Book Club choice; I've sold dozens of copies.

"I'll just need your receipt," I say.

He frowns. "It was a gift."

"I'm sorry, but we only accept returns or exchanges with receipts." I point toward the printed sign next to my register.

"You have copies of the same book right there." He nods at the display. "Can't you refund me your current selling price?"

I smile and stick to my guns, repeating the policy.

He exhales in frustration. "Where's your manager?"

"I'm the manager, actually."

Cue the usual response: eyeing me suspiciously as the wheels turn in his mind. This small, young woman cannot have any sort of actual influence or authority. I am in fact thirty years old and of average height, but I was cursed with a baby face that makes me look at least five years younger—which is why I dress professionally and always wear my hair up.

"I mean the head manager," he says. "Is he here?"

My smile freezes. "You're looking at her."

He huffs. "This is ridiculous. The book was—" He flips open the cover and points. "Twenty-nine ninety-nine! Plus tax! That's an absurd amount of money for a book."

My jaw tightens. The foil accents on the dust jacket, the deckled edges on the paper . . . it's a freaking work of art! This man clearly has no appreciation for the craftsmanship that goes into creating a beautiful hardcover.

"Sir, I don't set the prices, but—"

"I want a refund. Now. I don't have time to argue with a checkout girl. Understand?"

The words are a swift kick to my chest. I'm proud of what I do; my job is so much more than running a register.

"Oh, I understand," I say, my smile disappearing. "But if I give you twenty-nine ninety-nine—plus tax!—for a book that may not have been purchased here—"

"It was—"

"Even if I do sell it at some point, I won't make any profit.

Furthermore . . ." I take off the dust jacket and inspect the book; the spine is visibly cracked. "This book has been read."

"That's not—"

"So technically speaking, it's not in sellable condition." My hands shake as I hand it back to him, but I keep my voice calm and cool. "If I give you twenty-nine ninety-nine plus tax for this unsellable book, I will lose that money. And if I do that for other customers, I will not be able to afford to keep the lights on and replace the paper rolls in my register and pay my own meager wages, and eventually this store will close, and you, sir, will have contributed to the demise of one of Boston's most beloved literary establishments, a store that has stood in this spot and served this community for over sixty years."

He's flustered, pink in the face, and for a moment I think he's going to start yelling . . .

But then he wheels around and stomps away. Before leaving, he turns back and shouts, "I will never set foot in this store again!"

"We'll miss you terribly," I say.

"Bitch," he mutters.

My stomach bottoms out, but he's already gone.

Behind me, my sister slow-claps. "That dude just got Josie'd," she says, grinning. "It's been a while since I've seen that."

She must not have heard the last thing he said. I sigh, trying to shake off the nastiness of that final insult. I hate that I'm now questioning myself, wondering if I was rude. It's a constant tightrope act, running a business as a woman, wanting to be respected for my abilities but knowing that no one will take me seriously unless I'm nice.

"He was just . . ."

"Oh, he deserved it," she says. "But if you have the emotional energy, it may be useful to explore why you react like that when people disparage your career."

"Because it's incredibly rude!" Though of course, it's much

more than that. It's the fear that maybe they're right, that I'll never amount to anything of importance and I don't deserve this job anyway.

"Yes," Georgia says, "and maybe it's a wound you haven't fully healed yet?"

I purse my lips and remind myself that I am absolutely, positively thrilled that my sister is studying what she loves.

"You know what? I think it's time for coffee," I say, and head out into the early morning sunshine.

Beans is bustling. Eddie's new hire, Mabel, takes my order (an Americano for me, a dirty iced chai for Georgia), smiling nervously as she promises to get it right this time.

"Is she scared of me?" I ask Eddie, who's wiping down a table.

"No, she's scared of me. I gave her a lecture about not assuming someone's gender based on their coffee order." He gives me a concerned look. "You okay?"

I slump into a chair, the word bitch crawling around my mind like an ugly spider. "I had a terrible customer."

"Already? You're not even open!"

"I know!" I tell him the story, and he looks appalled. "It just felt so . . . belittling. Xander does the same thing."

Eddie gives my shoulder a sympathetic squeeze. "Try not to let the bastards get to ya."

Something occurs to me. "Wait—how does Xander's plan affect Beans?"

He shrugs. "My guess is I'll be working under the head manager."

I hear the disappointment in his voice. Eddie enjoys being in charge as much as I do.

"If I win, I'll make sure you get to keep running it the way you want."

He hesitates a beat too long before saying, "Thanks, darling."

Hang on. Does he not think I'm going to win?

"Eddie," I say, leaning forward, "what do you—"

"Oh, would you look at that line—I better help Mabel before she dissolves into tears."

He rushes back to the register, and I sit back, stung. Eddie's my friend—and he underestimates me, too? Maybe he knows something I don't. He's like the Mayor of Davis Square, keeping tabs on everything. He sees how many people go into Brian's store compared to mine and how many walk out with purchases. Meanwhile, I don't know much about Happy Endings. All I know is that the clientele is mostly women (judging by the customers I've seen holding pink and gold bags), and I think the employees are, too.

"Josie?"

I stand and run smack into a solid chest. A hand grips my arm to steady me. I look up; it's Brian.

He's shockingly tall this close—even with my four-inch heels, he towers over me. I have to tilt my chin way up, giving me a view of his jaw, covered in light brown flecks of stubble. The heat of his hand gripping my arm radiates through the sleeve of my blouse.

"Excuse me," I say, taking a step back.

He releases me and clears his throat. "Sorry. I was . . . uh, hoping we could chat?"

Today, Brian's wearing a gray cardigan, along with his pin-studded lanyard and tortoiseshell glasses. His hair's still a mess, though if he was a hero in a romance novel it would probably be described as flowing chestnut locks that partially obscure the piercing gaze of his mahogany eyes.

I'm not sure what he wants, but I'm not having this conversation while he's looking down on me.

"Sure," I say. "Let's sit."

He seems surprised, but nods, and we both pull out chairs. My eyes catch on another pin on his lanyard: WHEN I THINK ABOUT BOOKS, I TOUCH MY SHELF.

It takes me a moment to get it. When I do, the song by the

Divinyls starts playing in my head, sparking a memory: my mom, dancing around the kitchen, deep in the throes of another love affair with another man she swore was the One. Little Georgia, dancing along, hope sparkling in her eyes. Forgetting that in a few weeks, this boyfriend would dump our mom and she'd be back in bed, crying with the curtains drawn, forgetting that her two young daughters needed meals, clean laundry, and help with homework.

Shaking that away, I refocus on Brian. He's staring at me, his eyes drifting across my face like I'm a book he's reading.

A boring, bitter book.

"You wanted to talk?" I say.

He blinks. "Oh, yeah. About this whole Xander thing. I mean, there's no reason for us to be enemies."

"Agree," I say, though I'm wary. I'd love to feel like we're on the same side, united by mutual loathing of our evil boss. Unfortunately, it seems that Xander and Brian are bros, united in their mutual scorn of me.

What'd you call her store, Lawson? A bleak wasteland of existential dread?

"Great, that's great," Brian is saying. "Because, um, after Xander combines the stores, it's going to be a lot to manage and —and it's going to require a lot of work."

"Yes," I say, unsure what he's getting at. Does he think I'm not capable of it?

"I've been trying to think of what I could do . . ." He brushes his hair out of his eyes, hesitating.

"So you aren't out of a job when—"

"What do you mean, when?" My voice squeaks on the last word.

"I mean, if," he corrects quickly.

"You said when." I swallow the surge of dread. Did Xander say something to him? Maybe this whole competition is a farce and Brian's already got it in the bag? "Word choice matters."

"It was a slip of the tongue."

"A Freudian slip, maybe."

He blinks at me from behind his glasses. "Well, I apologize."

He doesn't sound apologetic. He sounds irritated, which isn't fair—he's the one who implied I was going to lose.

Exhaling, I glance at my phone. Almost time to open. "Thanks for the chat, Brian, but I—"

"Stop calling me that."

I rear back, shocked. "Excuse me?"

He mumbles something I don't catch.

"Hmm?" I say.

"Ryan," he says more clearly. "My name? It's . . ."

He turns the lanyard around: RYAN LAWSON. MANAGER, HAPPY ENDINGS.

My cheeks heat with embarrassment. I've been calling him the wrong name for days.

But before I can apologize, he stands. He's looming over me, a mountain of a man, and I scramble to my feet and try to muster a confidence I do not feel. "Is there anything else?"

"Yes, if you'd let me finish." He huffs out a frustrated sigh. "All I'm trying to say is that if I win . . ." He bites his lip, then blurts, "You could be my assistant."

Indignation sparks through me. "Your assistant?"

"I mean, I could hire you as an assistant manager so you wouldn't be out of a job." The expression on his face is all, See what a nice guy I am?

"Wow, that's great," I say.

"Yeah?" His eyebrows lift.

"I mean, you're the man, you should be the boss."

"Uh . . ."

"And all us little women should work for you, right?" I'm gathering steam, letting the frustration I didn't unleash on that awful customer surge out of me. "I bet that's why you love managing a bookstore. Hordes of women asking you to tell them what to read? And hey, if those books happen to reinforce the message that women aren't complete without a man, that's a bonus! Patriarchy at its finest."

"I . . ."

I step closer, poking a finger at his chest, saying what I wish I could say to every single person who has ever underestimated me.

"I'll never be your assistant, Mr. Happy Endings. And you'd better polish up your resume, because I'm going to win this battle. And the first thing I'll do? Fire you."

With that, I turn and walk off.

I wish saying all that made me feel better. Instead, I'm left feeling like no matter what I do, if I stay silent or stay in control or let everything out, I'll always end up in the wrong.

Like what you read? Pre-order the book as a gift to your future self! And if you email your receipt and your mailing address to AliBradyBooks@gmail.com before 6/1/25, we'll send you some fun book swag!

Find all the links to pre-order here: www.alibradybooks. net/botb

ACKNOWLEDGMENTS

This novella would not exist without a little inspiration and encouragement from our agents to have fun and try something new. Amy Berkower and Joanna MacKenzie, we are so grateful to have you on our team.

Thanks to Adam Brody and Kristin Bell and the creators of *Nobody Wants This* on Netflix for showing us that people DO in fact want fun and romantic stories about Jewish culture and traditions, and that learning about each other's traditions can help us all love and respect each other better.

Thanks to Ali Rosen and Mary Chase for being the world's fastest beta readers, Orly Konig and everyone in the Women's Fiction Writers Association Indie group for all the advice on dipping our toes into the self-pub waters, and KJ Dell'Antonia for suggesting we give Substack a try.

We are so grateful to Julia Whelan for making an author-dream come true. We can't wait to hear you and Teddy Hamilton bring Nessa and Jack to life.

Last but not least, a big thank you to both of our families who taught us the real reason for the holidays, and to all of our readers for being on this journey with us. You're the reason we keep doing what we do.

Merry Christmas and Happy Hanukkah!

- Alison & Bradeigh
AKA Ali Brady

ABOUT THE AUTHOR

Ali Brady is the pen name of writing BFFs Alison Hammer and Bradeigh Godfrey. They are the USA TODAY Bestselling authors of romantic, heartwarming, funny novels including *The Beach Trap, The Comeback Summer, Until Next Summer,* and *Battle of the Bookstores.* Their books have been "best of summer" picks by *The Washington Post, The Wall Street Journal, Parade,* and Katie Couric Media. Alison lives in Chicago and works as an advertising creative director. She's also the Founder and Co-President of The Artists Against Antisemitism, and the author of *You and Me and Us* and *Little Pieces of Me.* Bradeigh lives in Utah with her husband, four children, and two dogs. She works as a doctor and is the author of psychological thrillers *Imposter and The Followers.*

AN INTERVIEW WITH THE AUTHOR

This was a big surprise for your readers—a holiday novella!

A: It was a big surprise for us, too!

B: We've been playing around with another idea for a holiday novel for a few years now—but since we both have full-time jobs and have been on a book-a-year schedule with a new book coming out each summer, we haven't had the time.

But you had time now?

A: Well…I wouldn't say we had time. But we made time because this was something we were both really excited about.

B: We had the idea for this story at the end of October—and since holiday stories have a pretty short window, we had to move fast and do things a little differently to make it happen.

How was the writing process different from your other books?

A: Like our other books, we each had a character that we "owned." But usually, we have about six months to write a first draft. We spend a lot of time doing a pretty extensive outline and we know what's going to happen in each chapter. Our usual schedule is a chapter a week—we both write our character's next chapter and then swap and edit.

And you didn't do that for this one?

B: We didn't have time! We spent about an hour coming up with the basic plot for what we thought was going to be a short story. (We should have known it would be longer—we always write on the longer side!) From there, we took more of an improv approach, each of us writing a short scene from our character's point of view, then sending it to the other to write the next one..

A: It was like a literary hot potato! Especially one of Bradeigh's chapters. I was reading it and loving it—and when I got to the last line, she had one of the character's suggesting a game of strip dreidel. My first response was—OMG! I have to write a strip dreidel scene?!?!

B: You came up with that idea!

A: Yes, I mentioned it when we were brainstorming—but I was joking and I had no idea how it would work. But Bradeigh had written it in, so I had to figure it out! And I'm so glad—because it is one of my favorite scenes in the book. Super flirty and fun.

B: People are never going to look at dreidel the same way again… Things like that happened a few other times, too. In my head, Jack had a big family with a lot of brothers and sisters. But in an early draft, Alison wrote that he just had one older sister, so I had to go with it. Honestly, it made the whole writing process a lot more fun!

You guys did a really nice job of talking about the traditions of both Christmas and Hanukkah—do you both celebrate both holidays?

A: According to my DNA, I'm 99.5% Ashkenazi Jewish, so I have always celebrated Hanukkah. And for some reason, my family has always celebrated Christmas as well. Not the religious aspects, just the Christmas tree and presents. Growing up, my grandparents collected pigs, so our family tree was filled with pig ornaments. But that's a story for another day...

B: My family celebrates Christmas, it's always been one of my favorite holidays. I've never celebrated Hanukkah—but, speaking of hot potato—Alison ended her chapter right before sunset, so I ended up writing the scene where they lit the menorah!

Wow—how did you know what to write?

B: Google! I knew the basics, but I watched a few videos to get some more specifics. It ended up being a really special scene, and interesting to have it from the point-of-view of a character who didn't grow up celebrating the holiday.

A: You did an amazing job with it! I only made a few teeny tiny tweaks. I was very proud! And if I'm being honest—I had to Google a few things, too. It turns out I've been lighting candles the wrong way my whole life! So in a way, writing this book helped me learn more and connect on a deeper level with my own traditions. Pretty cool...

Did you work any of your own family traditions into the story?

B - Most of Jack's traditions come from my family–either things I did growing up, or things I do with my kids now, like wearing matching Christmas PJ's and reading The Night Before Christmas. We also celebrated Advent (not the calendar with chocolates, though we did have those, but the wreath with the candles we lit every Sunday in December). Some of my favorite memories of the Christmas season are of lighting those candles and reading the Christmas story with my parents and siblings.

A - I can safely say that I have never played strip dreidel before...but I've played the regular version of the game and try to have latkes at least once during Hanukkah. There were a few little things I tried to incorporate—like putting tinfoil under the menorah. But like I mentioned earlier, I had to do some research on the holiday. I learned the reasoning behind some things that I've always done (lighting the menorah by a window) and some things I've never done (lighting the newest candle first). It honestly gave me a whole new appreciation for the holiday and the traditions. The whole thing is really beautiful.

This book gets a little steamy... and this is your first pure romance, right?

B: All of our books (*The Beach Trap, The Comeback Summer* and *Until Next Summer*) have had elements of romance with open-door sex scenes. But until now, our books have had two different women as point-of-view characters, and while they each have a romance, it's only been a part of the story.

A: Our next book—*Battle of the Bookstores*—is our first full-length romance novel. It was really fun to write, and part of the reason we were inspired to write this novella. We wanted to introduce ourselves to more romance readers. And then hope-fully, they'll be excited to read our new book when it's out in June!

What do you want people to take away from this story?

A: Ooh, good question. A lot, honestly. I hope that people will approach this story and whatever holiday they don't celebrate with open hearts and minds. It's been a tough year for the Jewish community, and I think so much of the hate we see in the world comes from a lack of understanding. So I hope that this story makes our Jewish readers feel seen, and that it helps our non-Jewish readers have a better understanding about the traditions and the stories behind the holiday. At the end of the day, I hope people come away with a new understanding and respect for each other. I know, it's a lot to ask of a novella!

B: I've always loved learning about different cultures and

religions, and I hope readers who celebrate either holiday (or neither of them!) might learn something new. Like Nessa says in the story, traditions are like a thread that ties us all together, creating a tapestry of memories that connect us to our family, our cultures, or beliefs–and sharing traditions and beliefs can help us respect and appreciate each other. On a less serious note, I also hope readers find the story to be a cozy, fun, romantic escape–we all need that!

Okay, now let's talk about how you're releasing the story. Three different ways!

B: At first, we were talking about writing this short story as a free gift for our newsletter subscribers, to thank our readers for being such amazing supporters and friends through the years.

Where did the idea of releasing it serial-style on Substack come in?

A: When we were about a week away from finishing the draft, I recorded a mini episode for the #AmWriting podcast with Jennie Nash and KJ Dell'Antonia. After we stopped recording, I told them a bit about what was going on with us and the idea we had for the short story. KJ suggested releasing it in a serial style on Substack. I wasn't sure about the idea at first, but the more I thought about it, the more excited I got!

And you're also self-publishing the ebook and print book?

B: Yes! We've had a crash course in indie publishing the last few weeks, but we have a few friends who have done it before and provided a lot of helpful advice.

A: And we got a lot of help from the Women's Fiction Writers Association Indie Publishing group. That's actually the writing group where Bradeigh and I first met! They have a sub-Facebook group for people who indie publish and they were very patient and helpful answering a lot of our questions.

Now can we talk about how you got the queen of audiobooks, Julia Whelan, to narrate this book?

A: I'm seriously still pinching myself over that one. I'm such a big fan of Julia as an author and a performer, it's been one of my author dreams to have her narrate something I wrote.

B: The whole thing happened so fast—every step of the way, I was like—is this really happening?

A: We knew it was a long shot, but we've become friends with Julia over the last few years (which is so cool!) and as a big audio book fan, I love what she's doing with her new company, Audiobrary. (If you haven't heard of it, it's an amazing new platform that fairly pays both the author and the narrator. Believe it or not, most other companies pay narrators a flat fee based on the length of the book's recording, and the narrators don't get any additional money, even if their audiobook sells millions of copies.) Bradeigh and I both know how important narrators are, and we're thrilled to have our story on the Audiobrary platform—especially with Julia Whelan and Teddy Hamilton!

Before we finish, let's do a quick Rapid Round of Questions:

Favorite Christmas Song:

A: I want a hippopotamus for Christmas

B: I ADORE Christmas music, so this is tough, but my current obsession is Pentatonix's Twelve Days of Christmas, because it is so creative and fun.

Applesauce or Sour Cream:

A: Applesauce!

B: Never had either! Maybe I should rectify that this year?

Matching PJs—love them or hate them?

A: Love them!

B: I also love them!

Chanukah or Hanukkah?

A: Chanukah! (We spelled it the other way in the book so it didn't look so similar to Christmas since they both start with the same two letters.)

B: I have no preference!

Favorite Holiday Movie:

A: A Christmas Story

B: Home Alone or While You Were Sleeping

Thanks again for talking to us! Where can readers find more about you?

B: We're the most active on Instagram, @AliBradyBooks and via our newsletter on Substack: www.alibradybooks.substack.com